BULB-HEAD

BULB-HEAD

Carol Kasser

A Bubbie the Book Lady Book

iUniverse, Inc.
New York   Bloomington

Bulb-head

This is a work of fiction. All of the characters, names, incidents, organizations, and dialogue in this novel are either the products of the author's imagination or are used fictitiously.

iUniverse books may be ordered through booksellers or by contacting:

iUniverse
1663 Liberty Drive
Bloomington, IN 47403
www.iuniverse.com
1-800-Authors (1-800-288-4677)

Because of the dynamic nature of the Internet, any Web addresses or links contained in this book may have changed since publication and may no longer be valid. The views expressed in this work are solely those of the author and do not necessarily reflect the views of the publisher, and the publisher hereby disclaims any responsibility for them.

ISBN: 978-1-4401-8078-1 (pbk)
ISBN: 978-1-4401-8079-8 (ebook)

Printed in the United States of America

iUniverse rev. date: 11 / 6 / 2009

"No one can make you feel inferior without your consent."
Eleanor Roosevelt

This book is dedicated to all the bulb-headed children. In their honor, 10% of the royalties from this book will be donated to charity.

Acknowledgments:

My gratitude to

My husband Harris Biegelman who supported me every step of the way and provided computer advice since I embarked on this crazy career.

My children Rob, Jodie, and Stacy and their spouses Erik and Mike for being the best children any parents could hope for.

My grandchildren Hunter, Nichols, Dylan, Logan, and Kayla who are my loves and my inspirations.

My parents Marilyn Kasser and the late Arthur Kasser who taught me to love books.

Rita Cooper who suggested that I expand my short story into a novel.

Miriam Sunness who told me to explore the character of Tommy.

My teachers Marcia Stein and John Malone who encouraged my writing.

The entire staff of Highlights Institute at Chatauqua who stoked my enthusiasm and honed my writing skills.

Jonathan Maberry who taught me how to flesh out a story and more importantly, how to sell what I write. Every writer should have a mentor like him.

The children and parents of The Children's Alopecia Project for their insightful suggestions.

The authors at *The Writers' Coffeehouse* for their support and encouragement.

SCBWI and SSCBWI who showed me how to change writing from a hobby to a profession.

The librarians at Doylestown, Southampton, Bensalem, Abington, and Northeast Philadelphia libraries for their help with research.

The entire staff at Underwater World in Horsham, PA for sharing their scuba diving expertise.

The staff at Pennekamp Park for confirming facts for me and introducing me to a magical new world.

Matt Hendrickson and Beryl Wolk for their continued support for Bubbie the Book Lady projects.

Diane Bachman of the Bucks County Law Library for helping me research Virginia legal codes.

If despite the advice of these wonderful people, there are any mistakes, they are completely my own.

TABLE OF CONTENTS

PROLOGUE

Summertime and the livin' is easy
Fish are jumpin' and the cotton is high.
"Summertime" by George Gershwin

June 1962 was a time of shoeless, fishing-pole mornings and shirtless, swimming-hole afternoons. I spent starry evenings surrounded by the twinkling glow of fireflies, serenaded by chirping crickets. I was twelve years old. That was the summer before my voice changed, before I had my growth spurt. The summer IT happened.

But that June I didn't know what lay ahead. I celebrated the freedom of the school-free days with Ted and the other guys by playing stickball in an empty lot. Then hot and sweaty, we'd race to the swimming hole.

"Last one in's a rotten egg," shouted Ted. At the last possible second, I tore past him and threw myself into the water.

"Yep!" I gloated. "I can smell the stench from here."

"That's no fair. I'd a beaten you if Charlie hadn't tripped me," Ted grumbled.

"Yeah, and yesterday it was because the sun was in your eyes! What'll be the excuse tomorrow?"

"Oh, go suck an egg."

"Sure as long as it's not a rotten one, like you."

Life was good that June in the small town of New Hope, Virginia. In fact, things were good all over the country. President Kennedy made us think anything was possible. Then came July, when I turned 13, and IT happened.

SUMMER 1962: I

...July 1776 will be the most memorable epoch in the history of America. I am apt to believe that it will be celebrated by succeeding generations as the great anniversary festival....
It ought to be solemnized with pomp and parade, with shows, games, sports, guns, bells bonfires, and illuminations, from one end of this continent to the other, from this time forward forevermore."

Letters to Abigail Adams by John Adams

On July 4th, New Hope, Virginia celebrated with a parade down Main Street, followed by a picnic in the town park. The smell of cotton candy, steamed corn, and hot dogs mingled with the aroma of fresh-cut grass. Pa and I took part in the father-son baseball game. Just like at home, I pitched, he caught. We made a great team. Half the time, I could anticipate his signals before he even flashed them. Ted was my first baseman, and his Pa played second base. Tommy was there, dour as ever, in his dirty jeans, torn shirt and uncut hair. His Pa, unshaven and surly, snarled because he'd been put in the outfield, and then he played with a beer in one hand and a baseball glove in the other.

Tommy hit a three-run homer to put our team in the lead for good. He raised his eyebrows as if waiting for the punch line when I shouted,

"Nice hitting, Tommy!" I could have sworn he flinched when I raised my hand to give him a high-five. Then when he realized I meant it, an odd half-smile crossed his face. He muttered almost to himself,

"Good pitchin', Barry." My Pa was all over me patting me on the back, but I never saw Tommy's Pa put down the beer can to congratulate him.

We had tug of war and sack races, three-legged races, and wheelbarrow races. Kind of corny I guess, but I still liked it. I always loved July 4th. It felt like the whole town, no the whole country, was celebrating my birthday with me. Ma made two cakes for the picnic bakeoff. One big rectangular cake had blueberries in the left top corner, white icing, with rows of strawberries so it looked like an American flag. It said, "Happy Birthday America." The other was my favorite, a big round cocoanut cake with curved lines of chocolate sprinkles to make it look like a baseball. That one said, "Happy Birthday Barry." She won first prize for her entries.

When Ma lit the candles on my cake, the whole town sang Happy Birthday to me. Then the night capped off with fireworks. We sat on a blanket with Sheriff Jackson's family right next to us.

"Hello Barry. Happy Birthday! Are you having a nice summer?" asked Rebecca Jackson. She threw me that closed-mouth smile that brace-wearers use to hide their metal mouths. She had been in my class since kindergarten.

"Thanks. Yeah, the summer's been fine. What have you been doing?"

"My Girl Scout troop has been entertaining once a week at the hospital, and once a week at the Senior Center. It's fun. I sing a little." She pushed her glasses up on her nose.

"That's an understatement, Becky. You sing beautifully," the Sheriff bragged. Turning to me, he added,

"She's the lead singer. You've heard her sing in the church choir, haven't you?"

"Yes, Sir, I believe I have." To tell the truth, I'd never noticed that she was in the choir.

Rebecca's face was bright red. "Dad!" she said with an exasperated, half-whine.

"What? Aren't I allowed to be proud of you?" the Sheriff asked with the indignant air of a father who can't quite figure out what he has done wrong now. Then the fireworks began and further conversation became impossible.

The month started out so well, I wasn't prepared at all for what followed. By the middle of the month, IT happened! Not all at once. Slowly at first, and just a little bit, but then totally. Doc couldn't say why, couldn't say if IT would be permanent. That's when I took to wearing a baseball cap all the time, even when I went to the swim hole. Ted joked,

"Hey, Barry, do you even wear that cap to bed?" I tried to laugh. It was good-natured teasing, but I felt the knot in my stomach tighten nonetheless. What if Ted found out? What if any of the kids found out? IT became the focus of my life. Keeping the others from knowing became my main preoccupation.

That was the month I stopped going to church. Ma wasn't happy, but she understood.

"I just can't go, Ma. I can't wear my cap in church, so I just can't go."

"Son, I know you are upset, but it's not the end of the world. If you act like you don't care, the others won't care either." But that was the problem. I did care, terribly. The rest of the summer crept by in a fog of fear that I would always be some kind of freak, and that the other kids would find out. Then came August and another terrible tragedy. Marilyn Monroe died. Ma was glued to the news. Marilyn was only 36, the same age as Ma. Pa and I stayed by the t.v. set, too. The newsmen kept showing the shot of Marilyn standing on a vent with her skirt blowing up. Wow! What legs! Rumors swirled. Peter Lawford, the actor, and the President's brother-in-law, was on the phone with her when she died. Or the Kennedy clan had something to do with it because she had been involved first with the President and then with his brother, Robert. Or her diary was missing, and it contained incriminating stuff about important people. Or she'd been on drugs and booze. Her ex-husband, superstar Joe Dimaggio, cried in public. She was plastered on every magazine cover. I bought them all and papered my bedroom door with them.

I was kind of glad when September rolled around. School would give me something else to think about besides death and IT.

Summer 1962: II

"Summer's lease has all too short a date."
Sonnet 18 by William Shakespeare

On July 4th, Snake had one of his rare fatherly moments. He went with me to the town picnic. I wish't he hadn't. He started on the free beer early, and by the time the father-son baseball game began, he was soused. He made a scene, shoutin' and cursin', when he was put in the outfield. Every innin' he grumbled as he took the field, with a glove in one hand and a can of beer or a cigarette in the other. I stayed clear of him. I knew at any moment his volcanic temper could blow again. I din't want that explosion aimed at me.

I hit the homerun that won the game. Barry came up and gave me a high-five. It startled me.

"Nice hitting, Tommy," he said. I was waitin' for the sarcastic punch line, but none came. Folks in this town don't often have kind things to say 'bout me or Snake.

"Good pitchin' Barry," I muttered when I realized Barry meant the compliment. Then his Pa came up and gave me a good-hearted slap on the back. It felt kinda nice, like I was part of a team. Course, Snake never said nothin' to me. He was totally wasted. Snake thought the sack race games and stuff were for babies. He refused to take part, which was a good thing. I doubt in his condition he coulda stayed on his feet. His fatherly impulse over, he decided to find his cronies Killer and Weasel. I breathed a sigh of relief as Snake headed off. Never knew what I might do or say to set him off.

I coun't believe it when the whole town sang Happy Birthday to Barry. On my birthday, I don't get as much as a "good riddance" from anyone. I spent the rest of the day alone amid the laughin', happy families. I sat alone in a tree to watch the fireworks. Then I tiptoed into the house, careful not to awake Snake from his boozy sleep.

The summer passed too quickly. I stayed away from the house as much as possible. Some mornin's I spent fishin' in the crick. Many nights I passed sleepin' in my secret hideaway. Snake never noticed I was gone less'n he had chores for me to do. Once in awhile Old Joe from the movie would let me do odd jobs for him. I never told Snake 'bout that. He'd a taken the money from me if he knew I had it. Old Joe often let me sneak in to see the movies, too. Afore I knew it September was rollin' 'round. Din't much look forward to goin' back to school.

Back to School : I

"School days, school days, dear old golden rule days."
School Days, lyrics by Will D. Cobb

I was a little nervous as I entered the classroom on the first day of school. Even in 8th grade, I still got a touch of the first day jitters. I patted the baseball cap planted firmly on my head. This will be a good year I thought. I'm finally an eighth grader, and the eighth graders rule the school. And to top it off, I'm in Miss Jenkins' class. It has to be a good year.

Miss Jenkins had only started teaching at the school the year before, and all of the boys had crushes on her. Old Miss Walker, my 7th grade teacher, must have been a hundred. She had chin hairs, support hose, orthopedic shoes, and thick horn-rimmed glasses. She walked around cracking a ruler against the palm of her hand. And was she a shouter.

That's why I was happy to have Miss Jenkins. She couldn't have been more than 25. She had freckles across the bridge of her nose. She was always smiling. She really seemed to like us. I never heard her raise her voice. And she played music during class breaks. When I entered the classroom, Miss Jenkins was already playing the guitar. The kids were singing *This Land Is Your Land*. The music continued until the morning bell rang at 9:00. "Yup!" I thought. "This is going to be a good year."

Because the students were seated in alphabetical order, I got a seat in the front row, right next to my buddy Ted Cotter.

We had just pulled out our notebooks, when a tall, stern-faced man walked into the room.

"Good morning class. I am Mr. Stimson, your new principal. I'm glad to see you have your notebooks open. Before Miss Jenkins begins her lessons, I want you to copy down the new school rules I have initiated." He lifted the map that was covering the blackboard. The board was covered with 10 school rules. They were clearly not written in Miss Jenkins' flowery script.

1. Girls will wear dresses or skirts to school.
2. Skirts must be knee-length or longer.
3. Boys will not wear t-shirts or jeans to school.
4. Students will not wear hats or caps in the school building.
5. Students must have a hall pass to leave the classroom during school hours.
6. Only one student from any class may go to the bathroom at one time.
7. Students entering class after the 9:00 bell will get a detention.
8. Any student sent to the office for discipline will get a detention.
9. Any student engaged in violence against students or teachers will be suspended and may not return to school without a parent.
10. The use of cigarettes, alcohol, or drugs on school property will result in a suspension.

"Start copying!" Mr. Stimson gazed around the room. Everyone started writing except Tommy Thompson.

"You, in the back row. What's your name?

"Tom Thompson, sir."

"I don't see you writing. Are you waiting for an engraved invitation, Mr. Thompson?"

"I…I don't have a notebook." Snickers broke out around the classroom. Tommy's face turned red and I could see the vein in his temple begin to throb. He clenched his jaw. Miss Jenkins put her finger to her lips, and the room was immediately silent.

"I have your notebook and pen right here, Tom."

"Thank you, Miss Jenkins." The throbbing blue vein in the temple receded and the jaw unclenched. Tommy began copying. Mr. Stimson continued to glare around the room.

"You, wearing the cap in the front row. What is your name?"

"Barry Brenner, Sir." I could feel every muscle in my body tighten.

"You are breaking rule number four. Remove that baseball cap immediately."

"Mr. Stimson, I…"Miss Jenkins began.

"Miss Jenkins, I will turn your class over to you in a minute. I will handle this infraction. This is my school now and the students must follow my rules."

"Mr. Brenner, I am waiting. Remove that cap." I was frozen. I just couldn't take off my cap.

"Immediately, Mr. Brenner or you will report to detention after school." Wishing there was a hole I could drop into, I removed the cap, revealing my hairless head. Mortified, I slouched into my chair, as the room behind me erupted in laughter. I heard Tommy's voice in a stage whisper saying, "Barry the Bulb-head." More titters peppered the room. Mr. Stimson reddened.

"Uh, oh. I um… Miss Jenkins, I'll let you take over from here." The principal beat a hasty exit from the classroom. Miss Jenkins drew herself up to her full 5"3', put her hands on her hips, and stared the gigglers into silence.

"I have my own rules, and in this classroom, I am the boss." She smiled at me. "You may put your cap back on.

Rule number one: You will treat each other with respect.

Rule number two: You will treat me with respect.

Rule number three: I will treat you with respect.

Rule number four: You will get to know everyone in this class, not just your friends.

Rule number five: You will not judge each other.

Rule number six: You will do the best work you can do. Now, let's get to work."

I couldn't get my mind to function. My life was over. Everyone knew about IT. They laughed at me. Sometimes I worry about something, and then when it happens, I wonder why I ever worried. Not this time. This was worse than I'd ever imagined. By lunchtime everyone in the school would be calling me Barry the Bulb-head.

After the torment of the morning, I couldn't wait until the lunch bell sounded. I grabbed my book bag and ran out. After wolfing down my salami sandwich, I approached the boys playing baseball in the schoolyard. "Hi, can I play?"

Tommy Thompson snickered:

> Barry the bulb-head go away.
> Barry the bulb-head you can't play.
> Barry the bulb-head you must be brave.
> If I looked like you, I'd hide in a cave.

Tommy smirked at me. Then he glared around at the rest of the team. His eyes seemed to dare any of the boys to invite me into the game. I looked at my friend Ted. He bit his lip and turned away. I lowered my eyes. My shoulders drooped. I retreated to a nearby tree where I opened my book bag and took out **The Adventures of Tom Sawyer**. At first I kept glancing at the baseball game. But eventually I escaped into the book. Within minutes, I held my breath, feeling scared, lost and alone, as I wandered through the dark, winding cave with Becky and Tom. My fear grew with theirs as one by one each candle went out. When the afternoon bell sounded, I had to be shaken back to reality.

"Barry, Barry!" the voice shaking me called. Startled, I looked up at Ted. "The bell rang. We're gonna be late." I glowered at my best friend, the traitor.

"I'm sorry," he mumbled, "but no one crosses Tommy. He's so bad his own mother ran out on him."

Without a word, I scooped up my book bag and ran into the building. I didn't look back to see if Ted had followed me. I usually loved school, but I just couldn't concentrate that afternoon. I was on the wrong page when Miss Jenkins called on me to read. The kids laughed at me. When she announced it was time for math, I took out my Social Studies book.

When the class finally dismissed at the end of the day, I couldn't wait to get out of school. But as the other children filed out, Miss Jenkins whispered,

"Barry, come here."

"Yes, Ma'am. Am I in trouble?"

"No, Son. I know you are upset. I heard Tommy teasing you today, and I promise, I will take care of him. Will you be patient and trust me for a while?"

"Yes, Ma'am." I knew she meant well. But I knew Tommy. He wouldn't stop teasing until he was good and ready.

When I walked out of school, the baseball game was already starting. Tommy yelled, "Here comes Barry the Bulb-head." I changed my mind about playing, and trudged home.

BACK TO SCHOOL: II

"Readin' and writin' and 'rithmetic taught to the tune of a hickory stick."

School Days, lyrics by Will D. Cobb

I dreaded the start of school more than an old hound dog hates an encounter with a skunk. I was fourteen, a year older than the others in my class. Last year, I spent a week in detention for bloodying the nose of Jake Swenson who shouted "Tommy the skunk, why did you flunk?" It really made me mad, the teachers and the kids thinkin' I was dumb. I missed so much school the year my mother went away, I was left back. Then there were days when Snake beat me so bad, I wouldn't go out where anyone could see me. It warn't my fault. And it was hard to get the homework done when the power was out. But I was the school scapegoat. If something was missin', Miss Walker suspected me. And I'll admit most times she was right. But I hafta eat, don't I? If there was a fight, it was my fault. "The apple doesn't fall far from the tree," Miss Walker said. Din't matter that I was taunted. I threw the punch, I got the detention.

Then there was the scrape I got into with Beau Stuart. The little worm called me "Rag Boy." He deserved what he got. He looked like a raccoon when I got through wit' him. Finally, I got suspended for throttlin' an eighth grader who chanted, "Tommy, Tommy! Got no mommy!" If the teachers hadn't pulled me off, I'da killed that kid.

Old Miss Walker broke more 'n one ruler on my hand. But I just laughed. It drove the Old Bat crazy. My hand could break, but I woun't never let any of 'em see me cry. Besides I'm used to getting' knocked around. There ain't a teacher or kid in school who could come close to Snake when it came to deliverin' a whuppin'. If I could survive at home, there warn't nothin' I coun't handle at school.

Still, I din't look forward to another year of tauntin'. Although after the suspension, most everyone stayed clear of me. They thought I was crazy. Could be they were right. Maybe they'd be scared enough to lay off me this year. I looked down at the patched pants. I sewed 'em up the best I could, and I washed them in the crick. The water and electricity were off in the house again, so it was the best I could do. There warn't any bread in the house, neither. I pulled a few apples off the tree. They'd hafta to do for lunch. Snake must be off on a bender or in jail again. He ain't been home for a few days. Food and money's gone. If Snake ain't home by evening, I figure I'll have to fish for my supper. I din't have the supplies I was supposed to bring to school, and I din't have any money to get 'em. It was the first day, and I was sure to start out in trouble again, although Miss Jenkins was a decent sort, for a teacher.

Sure enough, I got to class and the new principal picked on me right off for not havin' my notebook. The class laughed at me, and I could feel my head start to throb. I knew it was gonna be another bad year. Then I got a break. The principal picked on Barry Brenner, and it turned out old Barry lost all his hair. I saw my chance. I chanted "Barry the Bulb-head" and the class laughed.

I felt kinda bad keepin' Barry out of the baseball game. He ain't a bad kid. And he's a real good pitcher. He never was one of those who laughed at me. Fact is, way back when my mama was around, Barry and me were friends. But if makin' Barry the class joke spares me, so be it.

BRAVE IN THE CAVE: I

"And the light shineth in darkness"

Gospel of John 1:5

"How was your first day?" Mom shouted from the kitchen.

"Okay."

"Come on in. I just baked cookies." I plopped myself down at the kitchen table. Mom poured me a glass of milk and sat a dish of cookies in front of me.

"How's your new teacher?"

"Miss Jenkins? She's nice."

"Well if your day was okay and Miss Jenkins is nice, why do you look so glum?"

"It's nothing."

"No, I think it's something. Why didn't you stay after to play baseball?"

"I didn't feel like it!"

"You didn't feel like playing baseball? Now I know something is wrong!"

"Tommy Thompson was there. He called me Barry the Bulb-head. He wouldn't let me in the game. Okay. Now will you leave me alone?"

"There's no need to be fresh with me, young man." Then more softly, she added,

"I'm sorry he teased you. But I love that bald head of yours. You are unique. You are different. You brighten my life. Wouldn't the world be boring if everyone was the same? Besides, when things get tough, that's when you find out who your real friends are."

"Yeah, and I found out I don't have any real friends. I hate my head. I hate being different. I want to be like the other boys. I want to be liked by the other boys. And I hate Tommy Thompson. He's a bully."

"That poor boy sure has changed a lot since his momma left. You know you boys were friends when you were little."

"Well I hate him now. He's dirty. He's always wearing the same patched old jeans and shirt. And he's mean."

"Son, you don't like him teasing you for what you can't help. Don't make fun of him for what he can't help."

"Great! He picks on me and you feel sorry for him." I stormed up to my room, slammed the door, and threw myself on my bed. I dozed off.

Barry Brenner, boy spelunker, stood at the entrance to Big Bat Cave with his class. All of the students lined up two by two, except for Barry. No one wanted to be his partner. Well, that's not quite true. Ted was going to be Barry's partner, until Tommy raised a fist and told Ted to stand next to him. So Barry stood alone at the end of the line.

As they entered the cave, the guide explained that the lights inside were only for the tour.

"Caves," he said, "are usually very dark. That's why the bats like it here."

"Bats? I don't like bats," worried Rebecca.

"That's okay. There is nothing to worry about. The bats won't come out while the lights are on."

"Ooh," said the students when they saw the giant stalactites hanging from the ceiling like rainbow icicles.

"Aah," they all said when they saw the huge stalagmites that grew up from the cave floor.

"You can walk around the columns", the guide said. "But don't touch them. They form when a stalagmite and a stalactite grow together. But they take hundreds or thousands of years to form, and sweat or chemicals from the human body can halt their formation."

Barry didn't even mind walking alone. He was fascinated by the cave. He studied each formation, trying to determine what minerals were responsible for each color variation. He felt a little like Tom Sawyer in the cave with his girlfriend. As the class wound through one room into another, he tried to imagine what it would be like to explore the cave in the dark. And then suddenly, he didn't have to imagine. The power went out! The room became pitch black. He heard Rebecca scream.

"It's okay. Be calm. I have a flashlight," the tour guide reassured them. He switched on his light. But then a startled Tommy bumped into him. The guide fell. He landed with a thud on the flashlight. Again the cave went dark. Barry could almost smell the terror in the room. He heard the rush of wings over head and his stomach knotted. Then an amazing thing happened. Barry's head began to glow. The bats retreated from the light. The children gathered around him to be close to it. Barry calmed his panicked classmates.

"*Don't worry. I can get us out of here.*" Barry started to sing his favorite church song: "*This Little Light of Mine.*" The other children began to sing with him. When they sang, they were not so afraid.

"*I think my ankle is sprained,*" said the guide. "*I can't lead you out of here. We'll have to wait until someone comes to get us.*"

"*I memorized the path when we came in. I can lead the class out and send help for you,*" declared Barry. Then Barry the Bulb-head led the class to safety. Tommy slapped him on the back. "*I'm glad you are Barry the Bulb-head. You saved us. I'd be proud to have you as my friend.*"

I awoke with a start. But I smiled when I remembered my dream. Next time Tommy teases me, I'll imagine him afraid in the dark cave.

BRAVE IN THE CAVE: II

"No light, but rather darkness visible."
Paradise Lost *by John Milton*

I came home from school and as usual no one was there. I rummaged through the house for somethin' to eat. Some peanut butter. No bread. Peanut butter and crackers'll hafta do for now. Maybe I'll head to the crick and catch me some dinner. Wonder if there's any squash left in my garden. It's too bad Snake won't let me plant in Mama's old rose garden. I sure could use that land to grow more vegetables. I can't find my fishin' pole. I wonder if Snake put it in the shed. I headed toward the first shed. Too late I heard noise comin' from there. Weasel musta been peekin' out the door as a lookout.

"Kid's comin'!" I heard him say. Snake came burstin' out the shed. "Boy din't I tell you to stay away from here." I could smell the moonshine.

"Killer, keep an eye on the goods while I teach this boy a lesson." He turned to me.

"I guess you need a night in the hole. One day you'll learn to lissen to me." He dragged me by the scruff of the neck up the path in the woods. He made me help him roll the rock away from the cave entrance. He cuffed me good once and pushed me inside. "I'll get ya tomorrow night. Now push from the inside and help me get this rock back in place."

I thought about saying, "No." I din't know as if he could push the rock back in place alone. But then I thought "Naw, it ain't worth the whuppin' I'd get." It was never a good idea to make Snake mad. So I helped him lock me in. When the rock rolled into place, the cave was as black as midnight on a starless night of a new moon. My mouth went dry, my stomach knotted, my breath quickened. "Breathe slowly! Breathe slowly!" I told myself as I felt my way along the wall to my secret hidin' place at the back of the cave. If Snake ever found out about my secret spot, he'd whup me but good. But he was too big to follow the narrow passageway, so my hidin' place was safe. I felt through my stash until I found my flashlight. When the light went on, the terror subsided. I liked puttin' one over on old Snake. He knew I hated the dark, so he thought this was the perfect punishment. But I'd loaded up the back with blankets and food and flashlights, and it had become my private place. I'd even made an escape exit out the back, so I could leave any time I wanted. Course if Snake ever came for me and I was gone, there'd be hell to pay. But if and his pals were makin' moonshine tonight, they'd be stoned tomorrow. Snake'd sleep all day. I figured I could go out my secret exit, go to school and be back before he ever came for me. I took my stick, rope, and matches outta my bag, pushed open my escape exit, and went to the crick to catch me some dinner. I found me a worm, tied him onto my rope, and afore I knew it, I had shad to eat. Used some twigs, matches from my bag and my makeshift fireplace, and cooked up a fine dinner. It was too cold to sleep under the stars, so I went back into the cave, wrapped up in my blanket, and nodded off.

I got lucky the next mornin'. I woke up on time. Usually I oversleep in the cave 'cause there ain't no light to wake me. Then I have to play hooky or go to school late and get a detention.

UNDER THE SEA

"Adopt the character of the twisting octopus, which takes on the appearance of the nearby rock. Now follow in this direction, now turn a different hue."

Elegies *by Theognis*

The next day, I was still sore at Ted. I didn't wait for him to come to walk to school with me. I biked down by myself. I parked my bike by the fence and headed toward the baseball field. This time I didn't ask to play. But once again Tommy started taunting me. There he was dirty, wearing the same clothes as yesterday, and he was teasin' me!

> Barry the bulb-head you can't play.
> Barry the bulb-head go away.
> Barry the bulb-head get away from me.
> You look like a monster from under the sea.

I think Tommy was surprised when I didn't lower my eyes and slink away. I gazed right at him with a grin on my face, thinking of the scaredy-cat Tommy in my dream.

"If I din't know better," Tommy said, "I'd think you were laughing at me, you little twerp." Still smiling, because I knew it infuriated him, I took my book and strode to my tree. This time, Captain Nemo and I were exploring *Twenty Thousand Leagues Under the Sea.*

That night, Ma, Pa and I sat in the living room watching *Sea Hunt.* Mom popped up some popcorn, and we sat together on the big sofa munching and watching.

"I want to learn to scuba dive," I told Pa. "I love the water. Maybe someday I'll be an oceanographer or a marine biologist."

"I think you are too young for scuba classes, but we can go snorkeling together when we go to Florida next summer for vacation. If you still want scuba lessons when you turn 16, I'll even take the class with you."

"Are we really going to Florida?"

"Yes, son. Your mother and I have been talking about it for some time now. We want to visit Key West and Key Largo. Your mother always loved that movie with Humphrey Bogart. So she wants to visit Key Largo. I am a fan of Ernest Hemingway, so I want to see where he lived in Key West. You read *The Old Man and the Sea*, didn't you?"

"Yes, Pa. I think I'd like to see Hemingway's house, too. And I read somewhere that there are a bunch of six-toed cats on his property. I think they'd be neat to see."

Ma broke into our conversation. "We'll talk more about this tomorrow. It's a school night. Give me a kiss and go on upstairs." I went up to sleep, my head full of Florida and snorkeling and all.

Barry Brenner, scuba diver extraordinaire, checked his air gauge. He had enough time for one more pass by the old boat. He swam down, fascinated by the sea life that had made a home on the reef near the sunken ship. The sea anemones waved in the water. The coral decorated the dull grey ocean bottom with oranges, pinks, and blues. The sea fan coral looked like purple lace. Brightly colored Yellow Tang swam in and out of the holes in the old ship.

It was almost time for Barry to surface. Then, in the distance, the peaceful sea world turned dangerous. An octopus had wrapped a tentacle around a diver who had accidentally trod on it. The diver was struggling fiercely and wasting precious oxygen in his battle. As Barry swam to help, the octopus let loose with a tide of dark ink. Barry was lost in the darkness. And a flood of questions swept through his brain. Where is the octopus? Where is the trapped diver? How much air do I have left? Which way is up?

Then in the darkness, Barry's head began to glow. The sudden light startled the octopus who released his prey. Barry grabbed the frightened diver and started upward. The panicked diver ran his finger across his throat in the gesture that meant his air was out. Barry knew they would have to buddy breathe to the surface. It was a dangerous maneuver. If they didn't pass the regulator back and forth just right, water could get into it. Barry had the expertise and strength to exhale water from the regulator if necessary, but he doubted the other diver did. He would share his oxygen, but first he had to calm down his companion. If the other diver continued to hyperventilate, he would exhaust Barry's oxygen supply, too. And they would have to stop to decompress before they could surface, so they needed to conserve oxygen. Barry patted the diver on the back and gave the thumbs up signal. He took two breaths; then he handed the regulator to the other diver. They had to buddy breath like that all the way to the surface. It felt like forever at the decompression stop, but Barry held onto the diver tightly to keep him from ascending too quickly. When at last they surfaced, Barry finally hazarded a glance at his oxygen gauge. The needle hovered just above zero. "Whew, that was close!" Barry told his comrade. When he took a closer look at the diver he had rescued, it was Tommy Thompson! "I'd of been done for if not for you," said a grateful Tommy. "You're a real hero. Thanks, buddy!"

Barry and Pa

A boy and his dad on a fishing trip—
There is a glorious fellowship!
                        From A Boy and His Dad by Edgar Guest

It was Saturday morning, 6:00 a.m., a red-gold-orange Indian summer October morning. Pa and I had our fishing poles slung over our right shoulders. Over my left shoulder, I toted my book bag with our lunches and my sketchbook in it. Pa was carrying the tackle box. We whistled the theme from the old Andy Griffith Show as we walked. I tried to match my footsteps to his. The grass felt cool beneath my feet. Pa let me go shoeless when Ma wasn't around. As we entered the woods, the leaves crunched underfoot. We got to the creek and unloaded our gear. I baited my hook and cast my line into the water. I sat on the small rock at the creek side with my feet trailing in the water. The brisk water warned of fall, even while the air temperature still said summer. I slid back onto the bigger rock next to Pa. It was a lazy day. The fish weren't biting. I propped my pole against the rock, and pulled out my sketchpad and charcoals. I glanced sideways and sketched a profile of Pa. When I was done, he took my pad. He smiled at what he saw.

"You're good, Son. You get better every time you pick up a charcoal. Will you sign the back of this for me and date it. Someday I'll be able to say I own a Barry Brenner original." Pa just had a way of doing that, making me feel good about myself. And that fall with my hairless head hidden under a cap, feeling good about myself was a rarity. But with Pa, by the creek, I hardly thought about IT. Just as I put the sketchpad away, my rod jerked. I grabbed it before it slipped into the water. I reeled it in.

"Shad," I said.

"Good job, Son. If we can catch a few more, we can have shad sandwiches for supper." We lapsed back into silence. But we never needed to talk.

The quiet was warm and comfortable. We only caught two more all morning, but it was enough for supper. We ate our peanut butter and jelly sandwiches, drank the iced tea, and lay back in a clearing looking up at the clouds. Then we started ambling towards the house.

"By the way, Son, I've got a little vacation planned for the family the first weekend of next month. We'll drive up to D.C. after school on Friday and stay overnight in Arlington. Saturday we can go to the Smithsonian. There's an airplane exhibit at the Arts and Industries Building that I think you'll like. Then on Sunday, I've got tickets for the Redskins' game."

"Awesome! Who are they playing?"

"Dallas."

"You're the best, Dad!"

"Speaking of best, let's play the game. Best baseball team."

"I wish I could say the Senators, but I have to go with the Yankees."

"Best Pitcher."

"Sandy Koufax."

"Best hitter."

"Mickey Mantle."

"Best football team."

"Green Bay."

"Best golfer."

"Arnold Palmer."

"Best basketball player."

"That's an easy one. Wilt Chamberlain!"

"Okay. Best basketball team."

"Celtics!"

"Best bowler."

"Don Carter."

"Best boxer."

"Sonny Liston."

By then we were home. Pa said,

"Let's clean the fish in the yard. Ma will have our heads if we make her kitchen smell like fish." By the time we were done, our hands stunk something awful, and Ma banished us to the shower. When we came down, washed and changed, the fish were cooking on the barbecue grill. We slapped them on a hamburger roll with some cocktail sauce and Ma made some corn on the cob.

After dinner, I went into the living room. Ma had framed my sketch of Pa. It was hanging over the piano. It made me feel sort of proud, kind of like a real artist. It was the perfect end to a perfect day.

TOMMY AND SNAKE

I never met this fellow,
Attended or alone,
Without a tighter breathing,
And zero at the bone.

                          From The Snake by Emily Dickinson

It was a Saturday morning, a rare, beautiful, warm October morning. Sunlight played peek-a-boo through the few stubborn gold and orange leaves that still clung to the trees. I wanted to take off and fish in the crick, but Snake left me a list of chores to do. So I raked the brown leaves that carpeted the lawn. For a moment I imagined Mama and me the way we used to crunch through them, or heap them in a pile and jump into them. But I snapped myself out if that right quick. No use thinking of Mama. She was gone. Then I weeded the vegetable garden. We won't get much more outta there this fall, I thought. Maybe a few more squash. I thought about cleaning up Mama's old rose garden, like I used to when she was still around, but Snake had forbidden me to go near there, and I knew better than to cross him.

I chopped some wood and stacked it by the back door. I didn't mind doing the outdoor chores, but then I had to go in and do the woman's work. I washed the dishes that had piled up in the sink all week. The grit was dried on. If only Snake rinsed his dishes before he tossed them in the sink, the work woun't be near so hard. But I knew better than to tell him that.

I'd heard Snake come crashin' in about 3 a.m. And the clothes he tossed on the floor for me to wash still reeked of marijuana. The old man would be mean today. At noon I finally took a break. I sat down in the yard by the woodpile, took out my notebook, and, hummin' to myself, I started writin'. Afore I knew it, I dozed off. I awoke to agonizin' pain in my left thigh. I looked up and there was Snake's boot comin' at me again.

"You lazy good for nothin' worthless kid. Din't I give you chores to do?"
"I did 'em, Snake. I chopped the wood, raked the leaves, did your laundry, washed the dishes."
"Din't scrub the bathroom though, did ya?"
"No, Sir. I'll do it right now." I knew that warn't on the list, but I also knew better than to say so."
"No, right now you run to the general store and get me some aspirin. My head is splittin'. You can do the bathroom when you get back."
"Yes Sir. But I don't have no money."
"Whaddo I look like, a freakin' bank? Now git!"
"Yes, Snake."
"And git me a pack of Camels while yer gone."
I limped the mile to the store. I palmed the aspirin without any trouble, but the cigarettes were behind the counter. I walked over to a kid looking at the comics. He was a kindergartener from my school.
"You know who I am, kid?" The kid looked up and saw my hands tighten into fists.
"Eh...Everyone in school knows you, T..Tommy," he stammered.
"Good. You're scared. You should be. You're gonna do me a favor, right?"
"Ssh..sh..sure.
"Walk to the back of the store. See that pile of cans in the corner? You're gonna bump in to 'em and knock 'em down. Get movin'." The kid scooted off, lookin' back over his shoulder at me as he neared the cans. It was perfect, I thought. When the kid knocked the cans down with a huge crash, even I wasn't sure if he'd done it on purpose or by accident.
"I'm sorry m..Mr. B..Brenner," the kid cried. "It was an accident. I'll pick them up." Mr. Brenner came over to him.
"No harm done, Bobby. Don't worry about it. I'll help you." Just then Bobby's mother emerged from the produce section.
"Bobby Jones, honestly! I'm sorry, Harry. I'll buy any of the dented cans."
"It was just an accident. No harm done."
While this exchange took place, I slipped behind the register, grabbed two packs of cigarettes, and walked out. I didn't much like what I done. Bobby was a decent kid and I had no call to scare him. But no one was going to beat him black and blue for it like Snake would have done to me if I didn't get him his cigarettes.

BOMB SHELTER

"Cry Havoc and let slip the dogs of war."
Julius Caesar *by William Shakespeare*

A few weeks after the fishing trip, my world was shaken to the core. Before that day, Tommy Thompson and my bald head were my biggest worry. After that day, I worried if I would ever live in a safe world again.

It was Monday, October 22rd, 1962. My parents and I sat glued to the television listening to President Kennedy as he announced that the Soviet Union had intermediate range missiles in Cuba, just 90 miles off the Florida coast. He announced "a strict quarantine on all offensive military equipment under shipment to Cuba." That scared me. A quarantine? Does that mean a blockade? War? The President kept talking and I became more and more scared. Then he said, "It shall be the policy of this Nation to regard any nuclear missile launched from Cuba against any nation in the Western hemisphere as an attack by the Soviet Union on the United States, requiring a full military response." War! Doesn't that mean war? I could hardly listen to the rest of it, but I couldn't turn away from the television either. Finally I spoke up.

"Are we at war with Russia?" My father tried to sound calm, but I could see he was worried, too.

"Not yet. But it doesn't look good, Son."

Later that night I couldn't sleep. I sneaked downstairs. I remembered the basement pantry that we rarely used. If we went to war, I would be ready. I'd have a bomb shelter all prepared just in case. From the linen closet, I carried pillows, washcloths, towels and blankets down to the basement. I raided the kitchen and filled the pantry with canned fruits and vegetables, soda, cups and plates, silverware, a can opener, peanut butter and jelly, and crackers. Just in case Russia really attacked, I brought in my transistor radio, flashlight, and batteries. I took some of my least favorite clothes and stored them as well. Then I went back upstairs, and slept fitfully.

When I awoke the next morning, my Mom stopped me.

"Barry, have you seen the peanut butter? I wanted to make your lunch, and I can't find it."

"Yeah, Mom. Can I show you something?" I took her down to my shelter. I really wanted her to laugh at me, to tell me I was over-reacting. The knot in my stomach tightened when she didn't.

"That's a good idea. It doesn't hurt to be prepared. I'll buy some extra juice, and we can fill some empty bottles with water. We can keep that down here, too."

School Daze I

There are those who teach only the sweet lessons of peace and safety;
But I teach the lessons of war and death to those I love,
That they readily meet invasions, when they come.
Lessons from **Leaves of Grass** *by Walt Whitman*

In school the next morning, Tommy Thompson forgot to tease me. All the kids were talking about war. Minutes after school began, alarms went off. This is it, I thought. War has started. Principal Stimson's voice boomed over the loud speaker. "All students are to follow their teachers in single file into the hallway, line up and sit down in front of the lockers, and await further instructions." Miss Jenkins looked pale as she led the class into the windowless hallway. The kids were absolutely silent except for Rebecca Jackson. She was crying. I patted her arm and sat down next to her.

Again the principal's voice crackled over the loud speaker. "This is an air raid drill. I repeat this is only a drill. We will be holding these drills every day until further notice. You may now return to your classrooms."

As we came back into the classroom, I saw Tommy slip out of the coat closet with a bag in his hand and slide into his seat. I thought carefully. Had I seen Tommy in the hall during the drill? No, I didn't think so. Miss Jenkins' voice seemed a bit shaky after the students returned to class.

"These are uncertain times and I know you are all worried. So am I. But President Kennedy will handle this crisis. That is his job. And we have our jobs to do also. So let's get back to our work."

A few hours later when we were ready to break for lunch Rebecca approached the teacher's desk. A tear slipped under her glasses and down her check.

"Miss Jenkins, my lunch bag is missing. I left it on the top shelf of the coat closet, and now it isn't there."

I knew. I just knew. But should I tell? Last week Jerry's lunch disappeared, and two weeks before that Carol's ice cream money went missing from her coat pocket. Miss Jenkins glanced at me. She saw me staring at Tommy. She put her finger to her lips. Oh, my God, I thought. She knows. And she knows I know. Why doesn't she do anything? Instead she said to Rebecca, "I just happened to bring an extra lunch today. Would you like a bologna sandwich?"

"Thank you, Miss Jenkins."

"My mother packed me six cookies. You can have three, if you want," I chimed in. Rebecca blushed slightly,

"Thank you. Do you want to sit at my lunch table?"

"Yes, thank you," I replied. Rebecca bounded back to her seat to put her books in her desk.

"Rebecca, um, I'll walk you down to the lunchroom." She smiled, and her whole face lit up. Something was different about her, but I couldn't put my finger on it. Then she beamed at me again, a big, full, white-toothed smile, and it hit me.

"You got your braces off."

"Yes, finally!"

"You should smile more often. You really look nice."

"Thanks." We walked into the lunchroom together, and sat down at a table. When I gave Rebecca three of my cookies, her friend Cheryl chanted,

"Barry and Becky sitting in a tree k-i-s-s-i-n-g, first comes love, than comes marriage, than comes Becky with a baby carriage." I was mortified, but Becky was really cool. She stared at Cheryl.

"Oh, grow up! Jealous, are you?"

Cheryl opened her mouth to respond, but a sharp comeback eluded her. She closed her mouth again. For a girl, Rebecca was easy to talk to. And she liked to talk!

"Last month, my Girl Scout troop sang for the kids in the orphanage. I liked it so much, now I go there once a week to sing or read to the children. Next summer I'm going to become a Candy Striper at the hospital. When I finish school, I want to be a nurse or a teacher. I like helping people. What do you want to do?"

"I love science and I love the water. I want to be a marine biologist or an oceanographer."

"Wow! I knew you were smart, but I never knew anyone who wanted to be an oceanographer."

"Next summer, my Pa's going to take me snorkeling. He says I can take scuba lessons when I turn 16.

"You mean like on **Sea Hunt**? I watch that every week."

"You do? That's my favorite show!" Lunch went so quickly I forgot all about shooting bottle caps in the yard with the guys. And for a whole hour I forgot to be afraid about a nuclear war.

School Daze: II

Not my enemies ever invade me-
No harm to my pride from them I fear.
Not My Enemies Ever Invade Me from **Leaves of Grass** *by*
Walt Whitman

I came to school this morning and everyone was talkin' about war with Cuba and Russia. I din't want them to know I din't know what they were talkin' about. So I jus' kep' my mouth shut and listened. Our power was out last night, so I din't watch t.v. Never turned my radio on neither. I hafta save the batteries. It was scary talk, though. Not that anyone would waste a bomb on New Hope, Virginia, but Washington D.C. was only 100 miles away. How far can a cloud of nuclear dust travel, anyhow? Wonder if my cave would be safe. Not that I cared much one way or t'other about dyin'. Ain't like life been such a joy.

We went into class and within minutes alarms went off. Got my heart racin' a bit, I'll admit. Ole Stimson got on the loud speaker and tole us to go into the halls. Kids were scared. Rebecca was cryin. I used ta call her "metal mouth" or "brace face," but I din't see the braces today. Now I'll hafta find a new nickname for her. Well, she still has those ugly glasses. Guess I'll call her four-eyed Mouse or Cry Baby. Anyway, the whole class lined up. Even Miss Jenkins looked white as a ghost. Figured no one would be watchin' me. Went to the back of the line. When the rest went out, I slipped into the coat closet. Opened someone's lunch bag and ate half a sandwich. Slipped the rest of the lunch into my pocket. If I'm gonna die, I ain't goin' hungry. Then Ole Stimson got on the speaker again to say it was just a drill. As the class came back in I slipped out the closet and rejoined the line. Looked around to see if anyone seen me, and Barry was lookin' at me funny. I glared at 'im. Hope he knows I'll whup 'im if he tells.

Come lunch time, the Four-eyed Mouse goes cryin' to Miss Jenkins that her lunch is missin'. I look at Barry, and he's headin' to Miss Jenkins' desk. I'm gonna kill 'im! I look at the teacher. Seems she shakes her head slightly and puts her finger to her lips. Does she know? I think she knows! Anyhow Barry stops. Miss Jenkins gives Rebecca some of her lunch, and Barry offers her some of his. When Rebecca smiles at him, somehow she don't look so much like a mouse. Never had any of the girls smile at me like that.

Then din't she walk to lunch with Barry and sit with 'im? Not that I'm jealous 'bout Rebecca. But I don't suppose any girl'll ever do that for a dirty, rag boy, thief like me. For the best, I guess. You care 'bout 'em like I cared for Mama, and they jus' leave ya. I ain't never gonna care for no one.

After school, Miss Jenkins takes me aside. Now I figure I'm in for it. But she don't yell. Jus' tells me she always brings extra sandwiches to school, and she'll be glad to share 'em with me anytime I forget my lunch. Shows me her school supply closet, too.

"Take an extra notepad and pencils if you want. Use it for your writing. Your grammar and spelling need some work, but you've got a way with words. You could be a good writer if you worked at it."

"Thank you Ma'am." I take the notebook and pencils. I look at the little grammar review book and dictionary. Miss Jenkins smiles and nods, and I take them, too.

"If you ever want to share what you write, I'd love to read it."

"Thank you, Ma'am." But I know I won't show her. I couldn't bear it if she laughed at my writing like Snake did. I'll hafta find a place in the house to hide these, so Snake don't find 'em. He thinks my writin' is sissy stuff. Does Miss Jenkins know I write stories and songs? She seems to know me, and she don't judge me. I won't steal lunches anymore, I decide. I don't want her to think bad of me. She's the first teacher ever tole me my writin' was good.

MISSILE CRISIS

"We've been eyeball to eyeball, and the other fellow blinked."
Dean Rusk, Secretary of State

After dinner, we planted ourselves in front of the television to watch the news. A grim-faced Walter Cronkite reported: "Yesterday President Kennedy announced that the Soviet Union is storing missiles in Cuba, just 90 miles off the shore of Florida. The President ordered a quarantine of Cuba to prevent any new weapons from reaching Cuba's shores. Today the OAS, the Organization of American States, voted to support the quarantine of Cuba. Cuba's leader Fidel Castro has declared the blockade an act of war. Russian Premier Nikita Khrushchev immediately asserted that Russia will defend its ally Cuba from any acts of American aggression. In response to these declarations, The President has raised our security level to DEFCON 2. This is the highest security level short of actual war. This is Walter Cronkite, and that's the way it is." Even when the newscast ended, we sat wordless, staring at the screen.

"Dad, what's Defcon 2? Does that mean we are getting ready for war?"

"Defcon is the Strategic Command Defense Condition. Defcon 2 is a very high level of alert. We already have ships headed into the waters around Cuba. Tomorrow, if any ships try to pass our military ships to go into Cuba, we may have to fight to stop them. So yes, it might mean war."

Each night we gathered in front of the television. The night of October 24th, Ma didn't even cook. We sat with our t.v. dinners to hear what was happening in Cuba. We learned that the Soviet ships, accompanied by submarines, had come right up to the blockade line. We had been minutes away from war. But the Soviet ships turned back at the last possible minute.

But things got worse on Saturday October 27. Pa wanted to take me fishing to get me away from the television. I couldn't go. The world was about to come to an end. I couldn't go fishing like it was just another normal Saturday.

I watched the news. I listened to the radio. Pa sent me out to rake leaves. I knew he was trying to distract me. But I took my portable radio out with me. To think a few days ago I'd been worried about losing my hair and Tommy Thompson. Now I was consumed with worry about nuclear war, mutual assured destruction, the end of the world. And all I could do about it was to make a stupid bomb shelter. The day passed slowly. Ted came by.

"Do you want to go to the movies? *The Music Man* is playing." I just looked at him as if he had two heads.

"Are you still angry because I didn't stand up for you against Tommy? I told you I was sorry."

"It's not that. I'm over that nonsense. I just don't understand how you can go on doing everyday things as if nothing important is happening in the world."

"I can't change anything, and neither can you. I can stay at home and worry like you, or I can go to the movies and forget for a few hours. I'm going to the movies."

"You're probably right. I wish I could stop worrying, but I can't." Ted left.

The evening news led with the following story: We came to the brink of war again today. An American U-2 strayed over Russian territory. Russian MIGs were scrambled to intercept it. Then American F-102 fighters were sent to guide the U-2 back to neutral airspace, and to protect it if the MIGS attacked. Fortunately the American planes made it back out of Russian airspace before the MIGS reached them. But we came within minutes of war. In an even more serious incident, a U-2 plane was shot down over Cuba. Military leaders are pressing the President to respond to that attack with military retaliation. The President has stated that any future attacks on our planes over Cuba will indeed result in American destruction of the SAM missile sites in Cuba. Meantime, Robert Kennedy has been reportedly meeting with Russian diplomats to hammer out an agreement to lead us back from the brink of war. We hope to have more on this development for you during our 11:00 news report.

It was Saturday night, and we didn't even go out to eat. And Ma didn't cook. We had t.v dinners again. I couldn't eat. The t.v. dinner tasted like cardboard. My mouth was dry. My stomach hurt.

"They shot down an American plane in Cuba. Doesn't that mean war?"

"Son, all the military leaders interviewed today are pressing the President to retaliate. If they have their way, it will mean war. The President's brother Bobby is still trying to negotiate a way out. I guess it depends whose advice the President takes. I wouldn't want to be in his shoes right now. We should know in the next day or two. But you worrying yourself sick over it won't change anything. We just have to pray."

Sunday morning, October 28, all the churches in town were having a pray-for-peace prayer service in the town park. I woke up and got dressed. Ma looked surprised and pleased.

"Are you coming with us this morning?"

"Yes! I guess some things are more important than my bald head. Besides, we're praying in the park, so I can wear my cap, can't I?"

"Yes, I suppose so."

Rebecca and her parents were there. She smiled at me, as she pushed her glasses up on the bridge of her nose. I smiled back. Every prayer we said had the word "Peace" in it. Never knew how many prayers for peace there were. Ted was right. There wasn't anything I could do about it. So I turned the whole problem over to God. I felt a little better, as if a weight had been lifted from my shoulders. And miracle of miracles, when we got home later in the day, the news said we'd reached an agreement. The United States had agreed not to invade Cuba and the Soviet Union had agreed to remove the missiles from Cuba. Maybe prayers really work. I don't know for sure, but maybe I should start going to church again just in case.

Halloween: I

*Men seldom make passes
at girls who wear glasses.*

Dorothy Parker

Ma wanted to know if I was going trick or treating tonight. I thought about it. It seemed kind of crazy after the week we just went through when I thought the world was coming to an end. Nuclear war to trick-or-treating in just a few days. We live in a crazy world! Halloween seemed silly and childish, but somehow normal. If the world was gearing up for Halloween, everything must be okay. I didn't have a costume. But when Rebecca asked me if I wanted to go around with her, I decided to go. Mom wanted me to wear my karate uniform, but that's not a costume. I didn't think sensei, my karate teacher, would like it. So I just took an old sheet, cut some eyes a nose and a mouth in it, and went as a ghost. When I picked Becky up and saw her in her princess dress, I was really glad I decided to go. Sheriff Jackson answered the door.

"Nice to see you Barry. I'm glad Becky has someone going around with her. I have to work tonight to make sure there are no mischief-makers. Have fun, but be sure to have her home by nine."

"Yes, Sir."

"And take a flashlight with you."

"Yes, Sir, I have one." We set off together. I looked at her.

"You look really pretty in that costume." She blushed and smiled. It gave me courage, so after a bit, I took her hand. I hope my palm doesn't get sweaty, I thought. We walked down to Old Miss Lipkin's place. She always made candy apples. Then we walked up and down Main Street. A little boy in a skeleton costume saw me and screamed. He ran to his mother. I recognized him from school. Bobby something. I took off my costume for a second and went over to them.

"Did my costume scare you? I'm sorry, Bobby. It's just me, Barry." I gave him one of my candy bars.

His mother answered, "That was nice of you. He's just scared because last year someone in a ghost costume stole his candy."

"It's hard to believe anyone in the town would be mean enough to steal a child's Halloween candy."

"Not all the boys in town are as nice as you, Young Man."

"Thank you, Ma'am."

I put my costume back on and went over to Becky. She took my hand. "That was a nice thing to do." We stopped in Pa's store, and he gave us apple cider to warm us up. Becky's cheeks were pink from the brisk air. Then Pa let us choose whatever candy we wanted. Becky and Pa seemed to enjoy talking, but I wanted to get out of there before he said something embarrassing. Pa handed me some money, and whispered "Just in case you want to buy Rebecca a soda or something."

"Thanks, Pa."

"Becky, why don't we see what Woolworth's is giving out?"

"Okay." She turned to my Pa. Thank you for the cider, Mr. Brenner."

"You're welcome. Stop in any time, Sweetie. Barry's friends are always welcome here." I cringed. "Sweetie," he called her "Sweetie!" I took her hand and fairly dragged her out.

"Your Pa's nice."

"Yeah, but I can't believe he called you Sweetie."

"I thought it was cute. My mom calls me that, too." I took her hand and we headed to Woolworth's. They were giving out penny candies. Becky got a sheet of candy dots. I got the candy cigarettes.

"Would you like an ice cream soda?"

"Sure. Do you want to share one?"

"Okay." So we sat at the counter drinking a vanilla ice cream soda with two straws. It felt sort of like a real date. I wondered if I was supposed to kiss her goodnight. Did I want to? "Yes," I was surprised to realize, "I do!" Did she want to? Are their rules for first kisses?

Becky sounded sad. "It's getting late. We promised my dad I'd be home by nine." I was shocked when I looked at my watch to see that it was 8:45. The time had really gone fast. I paid for our soda and we headed out. We had to walk at a pretty good clip to get to her house by nine. I held her hand all the way to her house. When we got to the door, I leaned in. She leaned in. It wasn't much of a kiss through my ghost costume, but it was my first real kiss. Hers too, I think.

"Do you want to go to the New Year's Dance with me?" I blurted out.

"I'd like that." She smiled. I grinned, too, although under that silly sheet, she probably couldn't tell. "See you tomorrow."

"See you." I ran all the way home. I felt good, and it wasn't just from all the sugar I'd eaten.

HALLOWEEN: II

Ghoulies and ghosties and long-legged beasties
And things that go bump in the night.

                         Anonymous Scottish Prayer

Halloween night! A cold, crisp, big-moon night! Last year I went out dressed as a ghost and stole candy from some little kids. They were scared. Some of them cried. Felt bad about it afterwards. Can't figure out why I didn't just go and collect candy for myself. I guess I thought I was too old for that. And since I was too old to celebrate Halloween, I guess I didn't want anyone else to enjoy it either. I egged the school, too, later that night. Still didn't feel bad about that.

This Halloween I didn't feel like scarin' kids. No point in stayin' home. We din't have any candy to give out, and no kids ever came to our house anyway. I read Miss Jenkins' grammar book for awhile. I been... I've been studyin' it every night. I wrote some in my notebook. Finally, I decided to go to the movies alone. Better not to be home if Snake brought Weasel and Killer back after a night of drinkin'.

The theater was having a whole night of horror movies. *The Blob! Them! Invasion of the Body Snatchers! The Fly! It Came From Outer Space!* Good movies all night long! I had no money, so I sneaked in. Old Joe, the ticket-taker always seems to be looking the other way when I come. Then, I got free popcorn and soda that the movie was giving out for Halloween. It was a pretty good night. I think I slept through some of the shows. Movies ended at 6:00 a.m. Walked home, looking over my shoulder, like the Blob might be comin' after me. Slipped into the house to change and get my school books. I managed to get out without wakin' Snake.

School Project: I

Have you not learned great lessons from those who reject you, and brace themselves against you? Or who treat you with contempt...
    "Stronger Lessons" from **Leaves of Grass** *by Walt Whitman*

Miss Jenkins began the class with announcements about our school projects.

"As I told you earlier in the semester, we will spend the next few months working on our term projects. I will break you into pairs, and assign each pair a state. You will work together to research your state, to write a paper on it, and to present your information to the class. You will be graded on the amount and quality of your research, the written paper, and the originality of your class presentation. Use your imaginations and creativity to make the presentations as enjoyable and informative as possible. Before you leave today, exchange addresses and phone numbers with your partner."

My mind was only half there as I thought about war, bombs, the bomb shelter, Halloween, Becky Jackson, and Tommy Thompson. But I snapped back to attention when I heard my name called.

"Barry Brenner and Tommy Thompson. Your state is Texas." No. Miss Jenkins wouldn't do that to me. She knew that Tommy was teasing me. It had to be a mistake! At lunch, I hung around her desk trying to get the courage to speak.

"Did you want to talk to me, Barry?" I took a deep breath.

"Miss Jenkins. I really need a different partner."

"Barry, believe it or not,..."

"Miss Jenkins," I pleaded. I was so upset, I actually interrupted my teacher. "Please don't make me work with Tommy. He's mean. He's a thief. You promised me you'd help me. You said you'd take care of him."

"I'm sorry, Barry, but you are breaking rules four and five for my classroom. You are not taking time to learn about a student you don't know very well, and you are judging a fellow student. Believe it or not, I am trying to help you. And I am trying to take care of Tommy, too. There are lots of things about him that you don't know. There are lots of things about you that he doesn't know. I really believe that the two of you will make a good team. Give it one month and if it doesn't work out, I'll let you work on your own if you prefer. Will you just trust me a little longer?"

"Do I have a choice?"

"No, I'm afraid you don't," Miss Jenkins said softly. "Tommy, come up here. Please exchange addresses and phone numbers with Barry."

I frowned. Tommy scowled. But we both did as we were told.

After school, Tommy was waiting.

"I'm not working with you. You do the research. You do the report and put my name on it or I'll flatten that bulb-head of yours."

"No, I don't think so," I whispered.

"What?" shrieked Tommy, hands clenched, the vein in his temple throbbing.

"No!" I repeated. "You want a grade for the research project, you meet me at the library tomorrow at 10:00. I'm not doing your work for you."

Tommy raised his clenched fists and took a step forward. Every muscle in my body tightened, but I looked him in the eye and did not back away. Without breaking eye contact, I pulled my middle finger back even with the pointer and ring finger and pushed my thumb against my hand.

"I wouldn't if I were you," I said softly. As the other kids gathered around, Tommy unclenched his fists.

"Aw, you're not worth it. I'd probably skin my knuckles on that bald head of yours.

> Barry the Bulb-head go away.
> Barry the bulb-head you can't stay.
> Barry the bulb-head you're a disgrace
> You look like something from outer space."

This time, though, the others didn't laugh. Ted looked at me with admiration. I did what he had not had the courage to do. I stood up to Tommy Thompson. And Tommy had backed down. I continued to look my nemesis in the eye. And then imagining Tommy the scared scuba diver, I smiled.

"I'll see you at the library at 10:00 tomorrow." The smile infuriated Tommy.

"Yeah, when pigs fly," he snarled.

Rebecca walked in step with me as I headed home.

"That took guts."

"Thanks." My adrenaline was pumping, but I felt good. I reached for her books.

"I'll walk you home if you want." She smiled.

"I'd like that." We just talked about school and stuff. Before I knew it, we were at her front door. Her Ma was in the front yard.

"Hello, Mrs. Jackson."

"Hello, Barry." I handed Becky back her books.

"Well, um, Bye. See you tomorrow." That was awkward, I thought. I'll bet she thinks I'm a geek. I wondered if I should have kissed her again. No, not with her mother there!

"You can come in if you want. I'll make us a snack."

"I'd really like to, but I have to get home. My parents will be waiting for me. I have karate class tonight, so we eat dinner early."

"Karate! Cool! I didn't know you took karate. That funny thing you did with your hand when Tommy threatened you. Was that karate?"

"You saw that? Yeah. That was called shuto, knife-hand."

"I thought you were going to hit him. Why didn't you?"

"I wanted to. I almost did. But sensei, my teacher, says karate is only for defense. If he heard that I took the first swing, I'd get thrown out of my class."

"Can you break boards and stuff?"

"Uh, yes. I'm testing for my brown belt tonight. That's right under black belt."

"Hey, look I found a penny. That's good luck. Wear it in your shoe tonight for luck."

I smiled. "Thank you. I'll take it with me. But I can't wear it in my shoe. We don't wear shoes in class."

"You break boards with your bare feet?" I could tell Becky was impressed.

"Yes, bare hands and bare feet. Well, I'd better go. Bye."

"Bye. Good luck." She seemed a little disappointed when I left. I wondered again if I should have tried to kiss her.

SCHOOL PROJECT: II

"His courage foes, his friends his truth proclaim."
Absalom and Achitophel *by John Dryden*

The day was goin' pretty good for me. Miss Jenkins gave me an "A-" for my writin' assignment. She said it was creative and imaginative and that the grammar and spelling were much improved. She read the paper to the class, and they clapped! I din't know whether to be pleased or pissed off at the looks of shock when she told the class I wrote it. Then when I was feelin' so good, she went and ruined everything. She handed out the assignments for the group history projects. She assigned me the state of Texas. But then, I couldn't believe it. I wasn't hearing right. Mrs. Jenkins didn't pair me up with Barry the Bulb-head. I knew he had seen me take Rebecca's lunch last week. I'da decked him if he told. But he din't, which means he's scared of me. Maybe I can use that to get him to do all the work. Still, I wish it had been someone else.

After school I told him, "I'm not working with you. You do the research. You do the report and put my name on it or I'll flatten that Bulb-head of yours."

"No! I don't think so."

Coulda bowled me over with a feather! I din't think he had the guts. There was something about the way his body changed that was menacing even though he never raised his voice. But he stared me in the eyes, and there was no fear there. I made a joke of it. But when I made my Barry the Bulb-head poem, the other kids din't laugh. Something changed. Because he wasn't afraid of me, the others were a little less afraid. I din't like it. Gotta respect him though. Din't expect him to show such guts. Think I might even surprise him and show up at the library tomorrow. And then I saw mousy, little four-eyed, Rebecca was all sweet on him. They walked home together. Felt a twinge of something. Again I thought 'No girl will ever walk home with me.

They're all afraid of me. Probly just as well. If my own Mama din't love me enough to stick around, no reason to trust any other girl.'

I went home by myself. No food again, but at least there was no Snake. Probably out on an early bender. He'll be vicious as a rabid skunk when he staggers in. I best stay outta his way. Found some of Snake's money stashed in his hidin' place. Took a ten. Hope he don't notice or there'll be hell to pay. I walked to the store and bought some milk, eggs, bread and cereal. Took some cold cereal for dinner.

KARATE KID

"Pilgrims of mortality, voyaging between horizons across the eternal seas of space and time."
Henry Beston, The Outermost House: A Year of Life on the Great Beach of Cape Cod

That night, I stood in the locker room at the karate school. I put on my clean white gi and tied my green belt in place. I was quivering with excitement and just a little nervousness. I was about to test for my brown belt. I bowed as I entered the dojo. The warm-ups took forever. Stretching, kicking over my head. Fingertip pushups. Front snap kicks, roundhouse kicks. The material in my gi snapped with each warm-up punch I threw. Then finally it was time to test. I moved through the katas almost by rote. Then it came to my least favorite part, breaking the boards. I threw a front snap kick. The board cracked in two. Then it came time for the hand strikes. I curled my fingers down tightly into my palm. I pulled the fingers back and thrust the heel of my hand forward in a palm heel strike. I focused on a spot just behind the board, envisioning my hand already there. I took a deep breath and struck as I shouted ki-ai. The board split. I gathered all my pent up anger at Tommy, and focused it into my hands. Board after board snapped under my strikes. With each broken board, I felt the rage diminish. The sensei commented on my fury.

"I wouldn't want to be the person you are thinking about right now. But whoever he is, you should thank him. I've never seen you perform so well."

"Thank you, Sensei." I put my hands at my sides, and bowed.

"Remember, Son, you never use karate to attack, only to defend."

"Yes, Sensei. But I have to tell you, I was really tempted to break that rule today."

"The fact that you didn't, shows me that you are ready for this brown belt. Now get ready to spar."

"Yes, Sensei."

I double-checked my equipment: arm protectors, leg protectors, cup. I was as ready as I was ever going to be. The sparring was a furious dance of kicks and blocks, punches and blocks, attacks and retreats. Strikes and split second reactions. Total focus and concentration. When it was done, I was soaking wet, and gasping for air. But it must have been enough.

"Congratulations, Barry! You showed real focus and dexterity tonight." Sensei bowed and handed me the brown belt. I bowed in return, never lowering my eyes from his.

I rushed into the observation room. "Mom, dad, did you see? I did it!" I waved my brown belt proudly.

"I saw, Son, but your mom had her hands over her eyes for most of the test, especially the sparring. I turned to my mom. I didn't even wince when she hugged me, although I admit, I did look to make sure no other kids were watching.

"I'm very proud of you, but I don't think I'll ever be able to watch. Couldn't you take up a safer sport like bowling?"

"Oh, Mom!" On the way home, we stopped at the soda fountain at Woolworth's to celebrate. I had a coffee ice cream soda. It was the first normal day we'd spent as a family since the end of the Cuban blockade. For a few hours, I didn't worry about anything.

I was way too excited to go right to sleep so I slipped one of my flashlights under the covers so I could read for a while. With Jules Verne's **From the Earth to the Moon** in my hand, I finally fell into a deep sleep.

Barry Brenner first astronaut scheduled to fly to the moon sat in his space capsule America 1 above tons of liquid oxygen, ready to ignite. Five…four… three…two…one. Blastoff! The force of liftoff thrust him back in his seat. The roar deafened those in the stands at Cape Canaveral, and the light from the burning fuel blazed across the Florida sky. As the capsule rose in the sky, Barry contacted the control center at Cape Canaveral.

"Canaveral this is America 1. The view up here is spectacular."

"Roger that. Take good pictures for us."

"Will do, Canaveral."

The flight went smoothly until an asteroid, really not much more than a small rock, glanced off the spaceship. The ship shuddered then lapsed into ominous darkness.

"Canaveral, we have a problem."

"Roger that Captain Brenner. We need you to check your instrument panel to assess the damage."

"*Negative. Can't see a thing. It's pitch black in here. Can't even find my way to the spare flashlights.*" *Just then Barry's head began to glow.*

"*Okay, Canaveral, I've got some light here. The computer is out, but all other gauges are within normal parameters.*"

"*America 1, we have a problem. Whatever hit the ship knocked you off your trajectory. You need to make a course correction or you'll fly off into space. We aren't going to risk a moon landing in a damaged ship. We want to re-orient you so you circle around the moon and then use that trajectory to catapult you back towards earth.*"

"*Roger that. With the computer out, I'll have to make the course correction manually. I need the new coordinates, Canaveral.*"

"*Captain Brenner, on my mark, ignite the fuel for 3 seconds. Maneuver the manual controls so that the moon remains in the window. Shut down the fuel when I say 3. Got that?*"

"*Roger Canaveral. Ready as I'll ever be.*"

"*Mark!*" *Barry pushed the fuel ignition button, and grabbed the manual control.*

"*One!*"

Barry mumbled, "*Sure could use another pair of hands right now.*"

"*Two!*"

"*This thing handles like a rusted out truck!*"

"*Three! Shutdown! Did you shut it down?*"

"*Roger that.*

"*Okay. I'm checking the trajectory now. Well done Captain Brenner. That was nearly perfect. Only someone with your focus and dexterity could have pulled that off.*"

The Cave: I

"Treat your friend as if he will one day be your enemy, and your enemy as if he will one day be your friend."

Fragment by Laberius

It was 10:00 Saturday morning. I was waiting at the library, and, of course, Tommy didn't show. I wasn't surprised, but I was angry. I went to the pay phone on the corner. I tried to call the phone number he gave me, but his phone was disconnected. He's not getting away with this," I grumbled to myself. "I'm not doing his work for him."

I looked at the address he had given me. I strode off in that direction, getting angrier with every step. I came to the edge of the woods and followed the path to the ramshackle house. As I approached, I heard shouting, and I dodged behind a bush.

Tommy's father was shaking him like he was a rag doll. His father's face was bright red, the veins in his temples pulsing.

"Where is it you thief? Where is my money?"

"I only took ten dollars, Snake. We were out of food. I bought bread, milk, eggs, juice and cereal. Here's the change." Tommy's face was white. His father took the change, and twisted Tommy's arm behind his back. The notebook in Tommy's other arm dropped.

"What's this? Wha'd I tell you 'bout wastin' time writin' your sissy songs? You fancy yourself a musician like your whore of a mother?" His father flung the notebook into the mud. "I think you need a few days in the hole to teach you some respect." Then his father cracked Tommy across the face. He went sprawling into the mud.

My voice quavering, I stepped out of my hiding place.

"Tommy, you're late. You were supposed to meet me at the library an hour ago to work on that school project. Let's go." Tommy grabbed his book and ran towards me. For a minute I feared that his father would come after us. He was quivering with rage. He shouted, "This ain't over boy" to Tommy's retreating figure. Tommy looked at me with awe.

"Boy, you are either brave or crazy. Nobody messes with Snake when he is on a rampage."

"You call your father Snake?"

"Yup. That's his nickname. Fits him, too. He's a snake if ever there was one. A rattlesnake. No, worse 'n that. At least a rattler gives you warnin' afore he strikes!" His eyes opened wide as if a scary thought had just hit him. "You gotta swear you'll never tell anyone what you just saw." I spit in my hand and said, "I swear."

Tommy looked down at his mud splattered clothes.

"I can't go to the library like this. Come with me. I'll show you my special place." We walked about a half mile into the woods down an overgrown dirt path. "This is the 'hole' my father was talking about. He and his cronies Killer and Weasel stash their moonshine and stolen property in there. The front is a cave, but I can't move the rock at the entrance to get in. My dad locks me in there whenever he gets mad at me. He used to just lock me in the shed behind the house, but now this is favorite place to punish me. He knows I hate the dark, and boy is this place dark when he rolls the rock in place and closes off the front entrance. Here we are. This is my secret entrance. Snake doesn't know about this." Tommy lifted a stone out of the path. He brushed the dirt away and revealed a big board. He pulled that aside and climbed in the narrow hole.

"You comin?"

I hesitated. Then I followed. It was a tight squeeze. Tommy went down the narrow pathway to a wider opening. Even with the secret entrance open, it was dark in there. I tried to imagine how pitch black it would be with that entrance closed off. He pulled out a trash bag containing a jar of water, a tee shirt and pants, some cans of fruit, a can opener, matches, a blanket, a flashlight, and some batteries.

"This is my emergency stash for when he locks me in here. My Old Man don't, uh, doesn't know about this part of the cave. I used to be terrified of this place, but now I love it. Nobody bothers me here. One time Snake put me in the cave and forgot about me. Must have been on a drunken binge, or maybe he was arrested again. I got desperate. I ran outta food and water. I felt my way along the walls, until I came back here. I could see a little light coming from above. I could feel air coming from somewhere. And there was a little mouse in here. I figured if the mouse could get in, I could get out. I used an empty can to dig myself this exit." As he talked, Tommy changed to the clean clothes. He pulled the clean shirt on quickly, but not so fast that I didn't see the welts on his back. I turned my head away as if I was studying the cave. I didn't want him to know I'd seen. We walked down another narrow passageway to the main part of the cave. He showed me the big rock his father and his buddies moved to enter the cave from the highway. We looked around at the stash that had been left in the cave. There was some jewelry, money, and some bottles of moonshine.

"Looks like Snake, Killer and Weasel, have been doing robberies again. This stuff is new." Tommy took a handful of twenties and stuffed them in his pants. "Stealin' from thieves isn't really stealin'" he said.

"No, but stealing from the kids at school is," I said righteously. Tommy bit his lip.

"I hafta eat same as everyone else. Besides Mrs. Jenkins always brings an extra sandwich just in case someone forgets lunch." It dawned on me that Mrs. Jenkins brought those extra sandwiches for Tommy.

We left through Tommy's exit. We carefully replaced the board, covered it with dirt, and placed the stone on top. Then Tommy went to the river. He placed his muddy notebook on a rock and wiped off the cover. He opened it and found the inside was still clean. He washed out his muddy clothes, and set them on another rock to dry.

"I love it here," he told me. "Sometimes when Snake throws me in the hole, I sneak out at night, set my blanket out, lie back, watch the stars, and listen to the frogs and crickets. I wash in the river. Then I catch me some fish, fry 'em over that fire (he jerked his head to the left) and have a fine old time." I walked over to the makeshift oven made with stones.

"You make this?"

"Yup. Rocks and mud. Lotta clay in the soil here. It makes a good oven."

"You can really take care of yourself. You're kind of like Huck Finn."

"Had to learn to care for myself. Ain't nobody else gonna do it." But he smiled, and I knew he liked the comparison to Huck Finn. It dawned on me that he slipped in and out of good English at the drop of a hat. I wondered if he even knew he did it.

While he was talking, I peeked at the notebook. Poems, stories and songs inside. Good ones, too. He saw me looking at the book and grabbed it.

"That's private!"

"But they're really good. I'll bet Miss Jenkins would put some in the school magazine." I opened my book bag and pulled out my sketchbook. I handed it to him. He flipped through the pages.

"Wow! These are great."

"I have an idea. If you submit one of your songs or stories to the magazine, I'll do an illustration for it."

"I'll think about it. Listen, it's too late to go the library now. And it's closed tomorrow. How about if we go to the library right after school on Monday?"

"Yeah, sure."

"Where will you stay tonight? You can't go home."

"I'll just stay in the hole."

"It's going to be pretty cold tonight. You can come to my place. I have a great fallout shelter I stocked in the basement, just in case. There are blankets and food and everything."

He followed me home. My mother was in the kitchen.

"Tommy's here. Can he have dinner with us?" If my mother was surprised, she didn't show it.

"It's nice to see you again, Tommy. It's been a long time. You are welcome to stay for dinner."

"Thank you, Mrs. Brenner." Tommy went into the living room. He saw the sketch over the piano.

"You do that?"

"Yeah."

"It's good."

"Thanks!" Then he stared at the piano. He walked around to the side. He bent down and looked at two small letters carved into the wood. T.T. All of the color drained from his face.

"Mrs. Brenner," he shouted. "This is my mother's piano. How did you get it?" My mother came into the room, wiping her hands on her apron.

"Yes, it is your mother's piano, Tommy. How did you know?" He pointed at the tiny letters.

"I did that when I was five. It was the only time my mother ever yelled at me. And then she cried. She loved that piano. Her grandmother gave it to her. Did you know my mother was a concert pianist before she married Snake? She taught me to play on that piano. How did you get it?"

"It was seven years ago, but I still think of that day often. It was 9:00 a.m. in October 1955 when I heard someone pounding on my front door. I peered through the peephole and saw your mom. She was absolutely wild-eyed.

"Maggie," I said. "What's wrong? You look terrified." She drew herself up and asserted,

"Mary, my name is Mary O'Shea. Snake renamed me Maggie, and I've always hated it. I've made a decision and I have to carry it out immediately before I lose my nerve again. I need your help."

"Anything I can do, just tell me what's going on."

"I'm leaving Snake. But I have to get away today. He's been in…. um… away, but he'll be home tomorrow. I've got to get packed, get Tommy, and get away from here before Snake comes home. If it were just me, I would stay. As my father said, 'You made your bed and you have to lie in it,' but Tommy deserves better."

"Where will you go?"

"I guess back to O'Shea. Believe it or not, I was once like royalty in that town. It was founded by my grandfather. My father was the Mayor, and the owner of a large furniture store there. And I was this child prodigy who had been accepted to Juilliard. And then Snake took over my life, and everything changed. When we eloped, my father threw me out. But he did say if I ever wanted to return without Snake, the door would be open. I haven't spoken to my parents since the day I left."

"What about when Tommy was born?"

"I wrote to them when he was born, but I never heard back from them. I'm sure they counted back the months, and figured out why I eloped. I guess they just couldn't forgive me. I mean in 1948, teenage girls in O'Shea just didn't… especially the Mayor's daughter. I couldn't tell my father what really happened. Snake said no one would believe me. It would be my word against his. And no matter what, I'd still be an outcast, unmarried and pregnant. What choice did I have? I was terrified of Snake, but I had to marry him."

"Oh, Maggie, I mean Mary, I should have known. I saw the bruises, but you never talked about it, and I didn't know how to bring it up. I wish I'd been a better friend."

"You've been a great friend. That's why I'm here now. I need your help. When I left home, all I could take with me was my piano and my violin. I can take the violin with me now, but the piano belonged to my grandmother. It is very special to me. If I leave it behind, Snake will destroy it just for spite. Can I leave it here? Once I'm settled, I'll send for it."

"Of course! I'll call my Harry and tell him you are lending it to me, so I can practice while you are on vacation. He can send some men from his store to pick it up right now. Can I do anything else for you? Do you need money?"

"No. I think I'm okay. When Snake was home, he took all the money I made. But since he's been away for the past year, I've been saving almost every penny. As soon as Harry comes for the piano, I'll take Tommy and go."

We hugged and that was the last time I saw her. But I knew something was wrong when she disappeared and left you behind. You were her whole life. Your mother would never have left you, if she had a choice."

"But she did leave me, didn't she? You said her parents didn't know about me. Maybe she thought they'd be more likely to take her in alone. I mean, I'd be a constant reminder of Snake."

"No, Tommy, you were the reason she finally got the courage to go. Something happened. I know it did. You were little. Do you remember that day?"

"Like it was yesterday! It was the day my life changed forever. I came home from school, and Mama was gone. Snake was ripping up her rose garden, destroying every flower, screaming, 'I can't believe that whore even thought about leaving me.' From then on I was never permitted to mention her name. He told me she had abandoned us. I was never allowed to go near her rose garden or the tool sheds next to it. He destroyed every picture of her I had. I can't even remember what she looked like."

"Wait! Your father was home? She didn't expect him until the next day. Do you think he did something to her?"

"Maybe… Yes. He could have. He hurt her before. He always said she belonged to him. He wouldn't have let her leave."

"I'm going to talk to Sheriff Jackson, again. I told him something was wrong when she disappeared. She would never have left you. But the Sheriff said your father told him that she just up and abandoned you and him. The Sheriff said he couldn't do anything more because your father never filed a missing person's report. Everyone just assumed she left him, and no one could blame her for that. As her son, maybe you get the Sheriff to reopen the investigation." Tommy nodded. His face was full of emotion, and he didn't seem to trust himself to speak.

"Wait a minute. I have a picture here of her with me when she was giving me piano lessons. Do you want it?"

"Thank you, Mrs. Brenner." Tommy turned his head away, but from my hiding place on the steps, I could see the tears in his eyes.

"And, Tommy, this piano is yours. Your mother only lent it to me. She meant to come back for it. So any time you want it, it's yours." He caressed the piano for a moment.

"I can't take it home. Snake would destroy it, for sure. But I sure would love to come and play it sometimes. Although it has been seven years; I'm not sure I'd remember how."

"You were good, really good. Your Mama bragged that at six, you could play *The Minute Waltz*. It'll come back to you. The song books are in the bench if you want to try."

I went upstairs. Soon I heard someone playing scales. Tentatively at first, then faster and more sure. Then I heard *The Minute Waltz*. I knew it wasn't my mother. She tried hard, but she never sounded like that. I peeked down the steps, and Tommy had his eyes closed as he played. I had goosebumps, and I didn't know why.

Later that evening, my mother asked "Would you like to stay here tonight, Tommy?"

"No, thank you, Mrs. Brenner. I'd best get goin'. Thank you for dinner." As I walked him to the door, I asked, "Why did you say, No?"

"I like your mother, but she's a parent. She'd have to tell Snake, and he'd never let me stay. Can I still stay in the basement?"

"Sure." My parents were in the living room. They never knew the door they heard open and close was the door to the basement.

The next morning, before my parents left for church, I went down to check the pantry. Tommy said, "I guess your family is going to church. I can't go. I went with my Mama when Snake was away. But it's all lies. God doesn't love me. If he did, he wouldn't have taken Mama away." I was tempted to tell him that I didn't go to church anymore, that I was angry at God, too. But it seemed foolish. I only lost my hair. He lost his mother.

Later that afternoon, Tommy was gone. He didn't come back that day. I figured he went to the hole.

THE CAVE: II

Snake was whaling the tar out of me when Barry showed up. That kid's got guts. Most grown men won't cross Snake when he's on a rampage. But Old Barry steps out bold as you please and says,

"You were supposed to meet me at the library at 10:00. Come on."

Even old Snake looked shocked. I grabbed my notebook, and Barry and I hot-footed it out of there. Then I had an awful thought. If Barry told the other kids about that beatin', my life wouldn't be worth squat. I can live with the kids hatin' me. I can handle it when they tease me, but I won't have 'em feelin' sorry for me. I'd never be able to show my face in public again. But Barry spit-swore that he'd never tell. Seein' how I treated 'im, that was pretty decent of 'im. I coulda told him so, but I din't. I don't do gratitude well. Haven't had much practice, so instead I took him to my special place. Never showed that place to no one else ever. He was pretty impressed with my hideaway. Said I was like Huck Finn. I liked that.

Then I saw Barry lookin' at my writin' book. My stomach tightened. Snake always laughs at my writin'. Calls it sissy stuff. I was waitin' for Barry to laugh, too. But he din't! He liked it. Even said it was good enough for the school paper. Then he showed me his sketchbook. Man, can that boy draw! He wasn't at all what I expected. But he really surprised me when he aksed me to stay at his house. Why'd he do a thing like that for me? No one else ever done nothin' like that for me.

His Ma was real nice. I couldn't help thinkin' bout when my Mama was around. Then I saw one of Barry's sketches hung on the living room wall. I admit I was jealous. It must be nice to have parents who are proud of you. I can't imagine the Brenners callin my writin 'sissy stuff.' Then I saw the piano and I was like to die. It was Mama's. I knew as soon as I saw it. There were the tiny letters T.T., I put there when I was little. My guts were turned inside out. I remember that piano. I remember listenin' to Mama playing for hours. I remember learnin' to play myself, even though Snake said piano playin' was for sissies. Mama said I was really good. I loved that piano 'cause Mama was proud of me when I played.

Mrs. Brenner told me how she got the piano from Mama. I think I always knew somethin' was wrong when Mama left. Snake told me, "Your Ma left you because you was too much trouble." Mrs. Brenner said Mama really loved me and she wanted to take me away with her to save me from Snake. Then she said the scariest thing: That Mama didn't think Snake would be home until the next day. I remembered Snake that day rippin' up Mama's rose garden and calling her a whore. And I knew. Like a kick in the gut it come to me. She din't leave me. Snake did somethin' to her. I thought my head would explode with the knowledge. And it was my fault. She was leavin' to save me. And I never said nothin' to the Sheriff when she disappeared. Maybe I coulda saved her.

I closed my eyes. And I did what Mama always did to escape the hell that was her life. I played the piano. As my hands raced over the keys I could almost feel her smilin' down at me. I'd get Snake. I'd prove what he did if I died tryin'.

The next morning I left for my hole. I had to be alone. Had to think. I hurt with a pain worse than anything Snake ever done to me. It was bad to think Mama had left me. It was worse to think she died tryin' to save me. I couldn't stand the ache in my gut. But I would find a way to get revenge. Then it came to me. If I told the Sheriff about Snake's moonshine, he'd be arrested. Then I could dig through the forbidden rose garden, and break into those locked sheds to see what secrets Snake had hidden there. Maybe one would be the key to Mama's disappearance. In my hole, I did somethin' that day I hadn't done in seven years. I cried. I bawled. I punched the walls and had the bloody knuckles to show for it.

When I left for school the next day, though, I had my tough shell on. Nobody would ever know that I could cry.

FEAR AND FRIENDSHIP: I

You gain strength, courage, and confidence by every experience in which you really stop to look fear in the face. You are able to say to yourself, "I lived through this horror. I can take the next thing that comes along."
You Learn by Living *by Eleanor Roosevelt*

Monday I headed off for school, anxious to see if Tommy was okay. I still wouldn't call us friends, but he'd really had it tough. I thought we had reached some kind of understanding. If Russia and the U.S. could have détente, I figured so could Tommy and me. But when I approached the playground, I heard:

> Barry the bulb-head go away.
> Barry the bulb-head you can't play.
> Barry the bulb-head you look like a mole.
> Why don't you hide yourself in a hole?

I looked at Tommy wide-eyed. I opened my mouth to protest, then closed it again as Tommy could not meet my gaze. I ignored him all day in school. When the 3:00 bell rang, Tommy approached me.

"Are we still goin' to the library to work on the school project?" I shrugged. We walked to the library in silence. I refused to speak. Tommy's shoulders slumped. He opened his mouth as if about to speak. Then he closed it again and lowered his eyes. We never said a word not related to our work for nearly two hours. To be fair, Tommy did pull his weight on the research. It was nearly dark when we left. Tommy started to head off towards his home.

"Where are you going?" I asked.

"I guess I'll take a chance on goin' home. Maybe Snake won't be there."

"Don't be stupid. He nearly killed you the other day."

"I don't have anywhere else to go, except maybe the hole, and it's gonna be cold tonight. I can't go back to your house after… after"

"Yeah, you were a real jerk. But you can still stay in the pantry."

"Why would you do that when I was so awful to you?"

"I don't know; maybe because I wouldn't wish Snake on anyone, not even you." Tommy almost choked on the words, but he said them.

"I'm sorry. It's just if I give the kids someone else to laugh at, they don't tease me."

I recalled the previous year when one of the 8th graders had called out "Tommy! Tommy! Got no mommy!" It had taken two teachers to pull Tommy off the kid. I was still angry, but I sort of understood. Tommy and I continued in silence down the alley behind the library. I didn't even notice the van parked nearby. Just as we got behind the bank, the back door flew open. Tommy grabbed me, and pulled me behind a trashcan.

"What are you doing?" I asked.

"Shh! Somethin's wrong. The bank shoulda closed an hour ago." We peeked out and saw two masked men carrying sacks. They pulled the masks off as they neared the van. Tommy gasped out loud when he saw their faces. The men froze.

"Who's there," shouted the one with the pock-marked face. "Come out wit' your hands up, or I'll start shootin."

Tommy and I slipped off our book bags and left them behind the trashcan. We came out slowly.

"Oh damn! It's Snake's kid. He can identify us."

"I won't say nothin' Killer. Honest." Killer and Weasel started walking toward us. Y'ain't gonna hurt us are ya Weasel? My Paw's yer best friend." Weasel turned to his partner. "Whatcha gonna do wid 'em, Killer?"

"I guess we'll dump 'em in the hole. We'll be long gone afore anyone finds 'em."

"The kid don't know nothin, Killer. Why don'tcha let him go?" Tommy asked. I looked at Tommy in surprise. He'd been such a jerk at school, and now he was trying to save me. I'd never understand that boy.

But Killer said, "He can I.D. us. He comes, too."

"Run!" Tommy shouted, and we took off. Weasel and Killer tore after us. Killer grabbed Tommy by his hair and wrested him into the truck. Weasel grabbed for me, but the hat slipped right off my bald head, and Weasel wound up with nothing but a handful of hat. I threw a powerful roundhouse kick that caught him in the solar plexis. The thief doubled over. Sirens sounded in the background.

"Damn we musta set off the silent alarm. Let's go. Leave da kid." Weasel staggered to the truck and Killer pulled him in. I gaped in horror as the van sped off with Tommy in it. I kept reciting the license number in my head 86243K 86243K 86243K over and over again. I repeated it as I ran to my book bag and pulled out my sketch pad. I scribbled down the numbers, then furiously began drawing sketches of Killer and Weasel. I had to get them right before my memory failed me. The sirens came closer. In minutes Sheriff Jackson and a mass of police cars blocked both ends of the alley.

"Barry, what are you doing here?" shouted the Sheriff.

"They took Tommy. They took Tommy."

"Calm down, son. Who took Tommy?"

"Them," I said handing him my sketchpad. "Tommy recognized them when they ran out of the bank. He called them Killer and Weasel. They're in a black van. That's the license number written on the bottom of the sketch."

"That was quick-thinking, to get the number. These sketches are good. I know these two. Petty thieves and moonshiners. They've graduated to the big time though with bank robbery and kidnapping. Did they have weapons?"

"The one Tommy called Killer said he had a gun, but I didn't see it."

The sheriff to his police car and put out an A.P.B.

"Be on the look out for a black van, Virginia license plate 86343K. Two suspects in a bank robbery Luke Killmer aka Killer and Timothy Dawson aka Weasel. Approach with care! They may be armed, and they have a 14-year-old hostage, Tommy Thompson."

Barry pulled on the Sheriff's sleeve. "I think I know where they took him. I know there's another entrance near Old Woods Road, but I only know how to get there from the woods behind Tommy's house."

"Okay get into the police car and show me the way." Sirens roaring, we took off followed by three other squad cars.

Fear and Friendship: II

In the fell clutch of circumstance,
I have not winced nor cried aloud;
Under the bludgeonings of chance
My head is bloodied, but unbowed.

Invictus by William Henley

I saw Barry approaching the schoolyard. He smiled when he saw me. I was afraid he'd say somethin' 'bout Snake or ask me where I went last night. Couldn't talk about it. Had to head him off. I stopped him cold with a taunt.

Barry the bulb-head go away.
Barry the bulb-head you can't play.
Barry the bulb-head you look like a mole.
If I looked like you, I'd hide in a hole.

He just stared at me wide-eyed. He opened his mouth; he looked kinda like a fish about to take the bait. Then he closed it again. I could see the hurt in his face, and I turned away. He'd been decent to me. I had no call to do that to him. But I couldn't chance havin' him ask me questions or talk 'bout Snake with the others around. Still I felt pretty lousy. Barry avoided me all day. Can't say as I blame him. When the 3:00 bell rang, I approached him.

"Are we still goin' to the library to work on the research project?"

He just shrugged. He still wouldn't talk to me. We walked in silence all the way. It felt real uncomfortable, especially when we'd talked so easy the other day in the cave. I tried to find the words to apologize, but I couldn't get them out. So I worked my tail off at the library. Kinda liked doin' the research. Hoped he'd notice that at least I did more'n my share of the work.

It was nearly dark when we left. I was headin' home. Figured Snake mightta cooled off by now. Then Barry did the strangest thing. I couldn't understand it, after how I treated him 'n all. He asked me where I was goin'.

"Home," I said.

"Don't be stupid. He nearly killed you the other day." I told him I didn't have any where else to go and it was gonna be too cold to stay in the hole. Then old Barry tells me I can still stay at his house. Man I nearly cried. I can deal with someone whuppin' on me, but I don't know what to do when someone is nice. I aksed him why he'd do a thing like that when I been such a jerk. Hope he din't notice when my voice broke. Finally got the words out to apologize. Tried to explain that I had to make someone else the class joke so I wouldn't be. He looked like he thought that over some. Don't know what he'd a said, cause just then we got to the alley behind the bank, and the back door opened. Been around trouble enough to know somethin' wasn't right. The bank shoulda been closed already. The van shoun'ta been there neither. Grabbed Barry and dragged him behind some trashcans. Shushed him when he tried to ask what I was doin'. Then I saw the two comin' outta the bank. They removed their masks and I saw Snake's friends, Weasel and Killer. I gasped out loud. Killer heard. He shouted,

"Who's there? Come out wit' your hands up or I'll start shootin'!"

I signaled Barry to drop his book bag. I did the same. Figured the cops would know we were there where the robbers were if they found the bags. We came out with our hands up. I know better than to mess with Killer when he says he's gonna shoot. He's the only son-of-a-gun meaner than Snake. He recognized me right off.

"Oh, damn. It's Snake's kid. He can identify us."

"I won't say nothin' Killer. Honest!" Then I tried Weasel. He was Snake's best friend and he weren't near as mean as Killer. "Ya ain't gonna hurt us, are ya Weasel. My Pa's yer best friend." I could see Weasel din't wanna hurt us, but Killer's the boss. He wanted to dump us in the hole. Weasel wouldn't cross him. I thought maybe I could save Barry. I figured I owed him, and I knew he'd get help for me.

"The kid don't know nothin' Killer. Why don'tcha let him go?" I could see Barry lookin' at me, mouth agape. But Killer wouldn't buy it. Said Barry could i.d. him. I shouted to Barry, "Run!" We took off but Killer grabbed me by the hair and wrestled me into his van. Weasel went after Barry. He grabbed for his head, but Barry's hat slipped of'n his bald head. Weasel stood there fish-mouthed when he seen he had a handful of hat and a bald kid standin' there. Then Barry up and threw the meanest kick I ever saw, and old Weasel doubled over. Just then sirens sounded in the distance. Killer cursed!

"We musta tripped the silent alarm. Let's get outta here. Leave the kid!" Weasel staggered to the van and Killer hauled him in. I looked back out the window and saw Barry jus' standin' there, starin' and starin.'

The van raced away, and I bounced around in the back like a ball in a pinball machine. My mind was racin'. Should I force open the back doors and jump? But the van was really flyin.' Was there anything on the floor I could use to hit Killer? I figured if I got him, Weasel wouldn't hurt me. I felt around until I found the tire iron. But Killer musta heard me movin'. He turned around with a gun in his hand.

"Stay still and put yer hands where I can see 'em, Boy. I don' wanna hurt ya, but I will if I hafta." I eased my hands off the tire iron and put 'em behind my head. No point in takin' the risk. If they put me in the hole, I could use my secret exit to escape. I'd hafta be careful tryin' to move the board with the stone still on it, but I done it before. Best to just play along with 'em.

Weasel and Killer pulled the van up to the front of the cave. They yanked at the rock until it inched out of place. Killer shoved me in. I staggered and fell, cracking my head against the side of the cave. I crumbled to the ground. Something was oozing down my face. I vaguely heard talking above the pounding of my head.

"Damn! Look at all that blood. I think ya killed 'im, Killer. I think he's dead."

"And we will be too if the cops find us. Let's go."

"We can't just leave 'im. It's Snake's kid."

"Trust me. In our shoes, Snake would leave 'im, too. We gotta get outta here now. "

They pushed at the rock, but they left in a hurry, before the cave entrance was completely blocked. When they were gone, I dared to open my eyes, and I could see a sliver of light filtering in through the entranceway. I tried to move, but my head felt like it would blow apart. "I'm gonna die here," was my last thought before nothingness.

THE RESCUE: I

"He who helps in the saving of others, saves himself as well."
Poor Henry *by Hartmann Von Aue*

The police car screeched to a halt at the entrance to the woods. I jumped out of the police car even before it came to a complete stop.

"We have to go on foot from here." I ran the ½ mile to Tommy's secret entrance with the sheriff puffing behind me. I tossed the stone aside, pushed the dirt out of the way, and lifted the board.

"Tommy! Tommy! Are you in there?" There was no answer. I started down the hole, but Sheriff Jackson grabbed me.

"Let an officer do that, Son."

"Sheriff, this opening is just barely big enough for me. None of your men will fit. And that's my friend in there. Let me go."

"Take the deputy's walkie talkie and my flashlight." You keep talking to me every step of the way. You hear?"

"Yes, sir." I wriggled into the hole.

"Tommy? Where are you?" No answer. I inched through the narrow passageway into the bigger area of the cave. Tommy was lying on the ground near the entrance. He wasn't moving.

"Sheriff, Sheriff!" I could hardly breathe! "He's here, but he isn't moving. Jesus, there's a lot of blood."

"Don't move him," barked the sheriff. "Is he breathing?" I moved closer.

"Tommy! Tommy!" He moaned, but he didn't open his eyes.

"He's alive. But he looks awfully white. He needs an ambulance. There's another entrance off the main road. Get some officers around to move the rock away from the cave entrance. It'll be easier to get him out that way." The officers swarmed around the area by the main road looking for the cave entrance. I stood by the partially opened cave entrance, trying to push the rock away.

"Sheriff, Sheriff!" I kept calling out. Finally the officers followed my voice to the entrance. They moved the rock out of the way, just as the ambulance pulled up on the road. Paramedics strapped Tommy to a board and hurried him away. The sheriff's cruiser, with me in it, followed the ambulance.

"We called your parents, but we'll have to stop to notify Tommy's father. His phone's out," the Sheriff said.

"No! You can't!" I stopped myself. I wanted to say, "His father beats him. See that bruise on his cheek. His father did that. Tommy's been staying in my basement so he wouldn't have to go home. And Tommy thinks his father did something to his mom." But I spit swore. I couldn't tell. I realized the sheriff was talking to me.

"Barry, I'm asking you again. Why can't I tell his father?"

"I can't tell you. Tommy made me promise. Just please don't call his father until you talk to Tommy." The sheriff must have heard the panic in my voice.

"Son, the law says his father has a right to know. If you have a reason why I shouldn't call him, you've got to tell me." I racked my brain. I'd sworn not to tell about the beatings, but I hadn't sworn not to tell about his mom, had I?

"Tommy just found out something that makes him think his father killed his mom."

"Your mother said the same thing, but there was no evidence."

"But you never searched the house or the grounds."

"We had no reason. Mr. Thompson said his wife ran off."

"Not without Tommy. My mom said Mrs. Thompson wouldn't have left Tommy. Just the other day, my mom and Tommy were talking about the day his mom disappeared. And some things just didn't add up right. Can't you search now?"

"I'd need a reason to get a search warrant. And she's been gone for seven years. What do you think I'd find now?"

"I don't know, but you have to try. Tommy has to know what happened to her. Tommy said his dad makes moonshine. Would that be enough reason to get a search warrant?"

"Yes. But I'd have to hear it from Tommy. From you, it's just hearsay. Let's make sure Tommy is okay first."

THE RESCUE: II

I felt a funeral in my brain…
A Service, like a Drum-
Kept beating-beating-till I thought
My Mind was going numb-

Emily Dickinson

Through a haze, I heard a voice calling my name, but I couldn't make my mouth work to answer. Where was I? I thought I opened my eyes, but I still saw only pitch blackness. My head was poundin', like someone was usin' a jackhammer inside it. Then I sensed a light moving toward me. My eyes flickered open again for a second, and Barry was there. I heard sirens in the distance, the noise compoundin' the bangin' in my brain. Someone pushed the rock aside, and the lights from the ambulance flared in. The glare caused spasms of pain in my head. Then the ambulance workers were strappin' me on a board and I was in the ambulance. If I coulda got my leaden tongue to work, I'd a begged them to turn off the damn sirens. The percussion section in my head was poundin' in rhythm to the siren's wail.

THE HOSPITAL: I

How many desolate creatures on the earth
Have learnt the simple dues of fellowship
And social comfort, in a hospital.
                    Aurora Leigh by Elizabeth Barrett Browning

When I arrived at the hospital, my mom and dad were there waiting. My mom was crying. She wrapped me in a bear hug. Embarrassed, I tried to wriggle free.

"Mom, you're squishing me." My dad extended his hand to shake mine, but when I took it, he, too, drew me in for a hug.

"Son, we were worried sick when you didn't come home for dinner. Then after the deputy called to tell me what happened, all I could think of was all the things that could have gone wrong. I'm very proud of you. Sheriff Jackson says you helped save Tommy." The sheriff chimed in.

"Your son is a hero. My police artist couldn't have done better sketches of the kidnappers. And having the presence of mind to get the license plate number! Even most adults would have been too rattled to do that. Not to mention crawling into that cave to find Tommy."

"Did you catch them?" I asked.

"Yes, the state police got them not more than twenty miles out of town. At this very moment, Weasel is spilling his guts to save his hide. To hear him tell it, you throw a heck of a kick."

Mom made me go to the snack bar. None of us had had dinner. I was still too wired to be hungry, but I ate some soup, just to stop my mom's nagging. She bought stuff to take to Tommy, too. It was well after seven before we were allowed to see him. My father stayed in the waiting room. My mother, The Sheriff and I went in. Tommy looked pale and small in the hospital bed. His head was wrapped in a bandage.

"How are you feeling?" I asked.

"I've got a hell of…excuse me Ma'am…. A heck of a headache. The doctor says I have a concussion. I have to stay overnight for observation. You'll get a laugh out of this, Barry. They had to shave part of my head to put in the stitches."

"Welcome to the club, Tommy the Bulb-head." He threw me a half-smile.

"I guess I deserved that."

"Tommy, I need to ask you a few questions? Are you up to it?" the sheriff began.

"Yeah. I guess."

"Barry said you knew the robbers."

"Yeah. Killer and Weasel. They're friends of my dad's."

"Some friends! They almost killed his son."

"Well, I don't know that my dad would much care. You didn't tell him, I'm here, did you?"

"No, but I'll have to. He has a right to know."

"No! I think he killed my mother. Are you gonna give him a chance to kill me, too?"

"Okay, son. Calm down. Tell me what you remember about the day your mom left. Mrs. Brenner here tells me your mom told her she was going to pick you up at school and take you back to her parents' house in O' Shea."

"She never came for me. When I got home Snake was there digging and destroying everything in Mom's rose garden, muttering about 'that no good whore.'"

"Excuse me, Ma'am," Tommy said to my mom, "but those were his words. He said, 'I can't believe that whore even thought about leaving me.'" After that he roped off her rose garden and chained off the two sheds in the back. I wasn't allowed to go near them. He beat the tar out of me when he found me trying to get into one of them. He told me that's where he made his moonshine, and I was to stay away."

"Okay, Son. I'll get a warrant to search the premises. I don't know what I'll find now, but I'll look. And I'll get an order from the judge to keep your father away from you in the meantime."

"Can't you arrest him now?"

"On what charge, Son? I can't arrest him for moonshining because I don't have proof yet. I can't arrest him for hurting your Ma for the same reason."

"Can you arrest him for beating me?" He opened up the hospital gown to show the bruises. "Barry saw him whalin' on me." My Ma gasped when she saw the welts. The sheriff looked grim as he turned to me for verification. I nodded.

"That's what I stopped myself from telling you before. Tommy made me swear not to tell." I realized how desperate Tommy was to find out what happened to his mom when he let us see those bruises. I think the sheriff knew, too, how much it took for someone with Tommy's pride to tell. I'd never seen Sheriff Jackson look so angry.

"I'll pick that snake up right now."

As soon as he walked out the door, Tommy said. "Man I wish I could be there to see this. Ya gotta go, hide in the bushes, and tell me how the Old Man reacts. I gotta be sure he's arrested 'cause I got plans. Come back first thing in the mornin' to tell me what you saw, and I'll tell ya my plans."

"But school…"

"Did you forget? Tomorrow's Election Day. School's closed."

The Hospital: II

Time that aged nurse, rocked me to patience.
Endymion **by John Keats**

At the hospital, nurses washed my head. Sure was a lot of blood. They shaved off a patch of my hair around the cut. I got 10 stitches, the doctor said. Then they did an x-ray of my head. Finally the doc came in and told me I had a concussion. Said I'd hafta stay overnight for observation.

"My head hurts like a son of a gun."

"I'll bet it does. You gave it quite a whack. I ordered some painkillers. They should kick in soon. Those headaches can last up to 6 months with a concussion. Bending, certain movements, bright lights, loud noise, can make them worse, so take it easy for a while. I'm going to wrap this bandage around your head. It will protect you from accidentally banging the stitches against the top of the bed while you sleep. There are some people waiting to see you. Are you up to visitors?"

"It's not Snake, is it?" The thought of him made my head swim.

"No, he's not there, just the Brenners and Sheriff Jackson. I'll tell them not to stay long." Mrs. Brenner came and kissed me on the cheek.

"How are you feeling, Son?" she asked. That brought tears to my eyes. Can't remember the last time someone did that. She handed me a brown bag.

"I didn't think they gave you anything to eat, so I brought you soup, a sandwich and some cookies. I brought these from the hospital's snack bar. Tomorrow I'll bring you something homemade."

"Thank you, Ma'am. That's very kind." Actually the thought of food made me nauseous. "My head's kinda poundin' right now, but when the medicine kicks in, I'm sure I'll be hungry."

The sheriff had some questions for me. I had trouble focusing, but I tried to answer. Then he said he had to tell Snake I was there. That brought me into focus in a hurry!

"No!" I shouted. Sheriff insisted, and I had to give him a reason to arrest Snake. I tried tellin' him about Snake killin' my ma and moonshinin,' but he needed proof. I had to get Snake in jail, 'cause I had plans. I was desperate. I heard my Mom's words from long ago, "You don't air your dirty laundry in public." "Sorry, Ma," I thought. "I have to, for you. I gotta get that Snake outta the way so I can figure out what he did to you." I lifted my hospital gown and showed the Sheriff my bruises.

"Can you arrest him for that? Barry saw him beat me." Sheriff's face got serious. Especially when Barry said,

"That's what I wanted to tell you. But Tommy made me swear not to." Barry's a good guy. He kept my secret, even after I was such a bad friend to him. Getting' groggy. The medicine must be workin'. Doctor peeked in.

"That's enough for one night. He needs to sleep."

Sheriff, said, "That's okay. I'm leaving. I'm going to pick up that no good, child-beating Snake." I signaled Barry to wait.

"Wish I could be there to see Snake get his. Ya gotta go for me. I gotta know for sure that he was arrested. Come first thing tomorrow. I got plans and I need your help." Barry promised. He looked tired and I felt bad askin', but I knew he'd do it for me. It dawned on me we were friends, and I didn't know quite when that had happened. Hadn't had a friend in a long time; wasn't sure I knew how to be one, but Barry sure did. Tired. Head hurts. Really sleepy.

ARRESTED!

A rat surrendered here
A brief career of Cheer
And Fraud and Fear.

Emily Dickinson

It was late, nearly nine o'clock, when my parents and I left the hospital. They weren't happy about driving out to the Thompson place at that time of night, but I had promised Tommy. Dad parked the car a ways down the road, and pulled off the path. We waited until the sheriff's car drove by. Then dad and I got out, hid behind the bushes where I'd seen Snake beating Tommy, and watched the whole thing. I wanted to report every detail to Tommy. Snake was in the yard, just locking up one of the sheds when the police car pulled up. Snake was startled. Then he was livid. He screeched,

"Get out! This is my property. You have no right to be here." The Sheriff slapped the handcuffs on Snake. He wasn't any too gentle about it either. "You are being arrested on child abuse and child neglect charges. You have the right to remain silent. Anything you say can and will be used against you in a court of law. You have the right to an attorney…" Snake fumed.

"I know my damn rights! And whatever that rotten kid told you, he's lyin'. He's no good, just like his mother."

"Tell it to the judge," said the deputy.

"And as soon as I get a search warrant, and a search dog, I'll be back here to scour these grounds from top to bottom. I think I'll start with that shed you just left," the Sheriff added.

"You stay outta there! That is private property. You got no right," shrieked Snake.

"As soon as I have that warrant, I will have the right," replied the Sheriff. To his deputy, he said, "Get that creep out of my sight. I saw the boy's bruises. If I take him in, I'm afraid my billy club might get a mind of its own. Take him to the station and book him." Snake was driven off still fuming and cursing as he went.

DIGGING IN THE GARDEN: I

"The snake stood up for evil in the garden."
                    The Ax-Helve by   Robert Frost

I went back early the next morning to the hospital to tell Tommy about Snake's arrest. It was the first time I saw him smile all year.

"Now Barry," he said. "Here's what we gotta do. The Sheriff has to wait to get a search warrant, but I don't. And I know where to look. Today's Election Day. School's closed. Court's closed, too. Means Snake can't a bail hearing until Wednesday. Unless the Sheriff gets Judge Jamison to sign the search warrant today special, I don't think he can get one until tomorrow. We gotta search before Snake gets released or he'll make sure there's nothing to find."

"But doesn't the doctor have to see you before you get released?"

"He only said I had to stay overnight. I stayed overnight. I can't wait till he releases me 'cause they won't release me 'cept into the custody of an adult. Sure don't wanna be released to Snake tomorrow and there ain't anyone else. So I gotta just go."

We sneaked down the back stairs. I brought my bike around. Tommy rode on the handlebars. I knew he was hurting. He tightened his grip on the handlebars every time we hit a bump. I remembered when I got hit in the head with a baseball. For months after, any quick movement or bending caused vicious headaches. I tried to avoid jostling him, but on that old dirt path, it was impossible to avoid the bumps. Tommy's knuckles were white, but he never said a word.

Even thought I knew Snake was in jail, I admit to butterflies in my stomach as we entered his yard. Tommy wanted to start digging in the rose garden. We took our shovels to the hard November ground. Tommy was shaky. I just knew his head was pounding. Sometimes his face would go white and he would drop the shovel and hold his head in his hands. I'd grab his shovel and hand it to him, before he tried to bend over to get it. With dogged determination, he'd take the shovel and begin again. I was tired, exhausted, but in the face of his courage, I couldn't quit. Finally, his shovel hit something. He dropped to the ground to dig it out with his hands. I could feel his pain, but I didn't know whether it came from his head or his gut. I know mine was knotted at the thought of what we might find, but that was his mother we were digging for. I could only imagine what he felt. At last we uncovered the object. A violin case. Tom hugged it as if it were a child.

"Ma's violin. Now I know she never left here." He placed it gently on the ground and we both started digging again. My shovel hit something else. Again we both dropped to our knees to uncover it. A suitcase. A big one. We held our breath as Tommy opened it. We released a combined exhale of relief when it contained clothes. He picked up a white dress.

"I remember my mama wearing this. It was her favorite. Her red hair pulled back by a white headband. She was beautiful." He held it to his face as if hoping he could inhale her scent from it. He was lost in his memories. His raw emotions were written on his face. I felt like an intruder. After a very long moment, he returned to the present.

"She isn't here in the garden, but I have to find her. I just know he's got her body on these grounds somewhere." Suddenly I remembered Snake's expression when the police discovered him returning from the shed. I thought about the look on his face. It wasn't fury. It was fear.

"Tommy, the sheds!" Tommy ran into the house. He looked for the keys Snake had told him never to touch. They weren't there. He ran from place to place searching. No keys.

Finally I remembered something.

"He was coming from the sheds the night the police arrested him. That's why he was so wild when the police arrived. He probably had the keys on him when he was arrested. They must be with his possessions at the police station."

Tommy went into Snake's toolbox and grabbed a hammer, and some tools I'd never seen before. He wielded those tools like a professional and within minutes the locks to the first shed were on the ground. We swung the door open and came face to face with Snake's moonshine operation. There was a still and bottles and bottles of moonshine liquor.

"Well, at least the sheriff will be able to hold Snake on moonshine charges. Say, how'd you learn to pick a lock like that?" I asked.

"One of the few things I ever learned from watching Snake."

As we approached the second shed, a terrible stench greeted us. I gagged.

"I don't like the smell of this. Quick get those tools." Just as Tommy had picked the locks, and the chains slipped free, the sheriff's car pulled into the yard.

"Freeze boys! Step away from there. I'll take it from here. You're contaminating the evidence. Deputy, please escort these boys to the police car." From my seat in the police car I could see into the shed. And what I saw will haunt me forever. I didn't want to look, but I couldn't tear my eyes away. Tommy's view, thankfully, was blocked by the deputy. As the sheriff opened the door to the shed, he gasped in horror. On one side was a pile of human waste. In the middle were empty food cans, and bottles of water. And there, cowering in the corner, red peach fuzz for hair, mostly skin and bones, was Mrs. Thompson. She shaded her eyes from the glare of the sun. The sheriff's walkie talkie was on, and we could hear every word.

"It's okay. You can come out, Mrs. Thompson. You're safe now." But she backed against the wall, keening in fear.

"Go away. You don't know what you've done. I have to stay. He'll kill Tommy if I leave."

Tommy buried his head in his hands. I heard a sob escape. I didn't know whether it was because she was alive, or because even now she was trying to protect him. My gut ached for her. My gut ached for him. And I knew the worst thing I could do was let him know that.

"We've got Snake locked up, Ma'am. He'll never hurt you or Tommy again."

"Where's Tommy? I don't want him to see me like this."

"Okay. I'll have my deputy take him to the hospital. He can see you there after we get you checked out and cleaned up. Deputy, I know you hear me. Get those kids out of here and to the hospital."

"Roger, Sheriff." The engine started and still I couldn't pull my eyes away from the shed. The red-haired skeleton tried to stand up, but slipped back down. The sheriff scooped her up in his arms. And then the car pulled away and I couldn't see her any more, but the image of her was emblazoned on my brain. We could still hear though.

"Oh Lord," the sheriff wept, "I haven't seen anything like this since I marched in with the troops to free the camp at Buchenwald. And I never thought to see the like again in my own town. I'm truly sorry, Ma'am. I should have investigated better when you disappeared. I'm so sorry."

DIGGING IN THE GARDEN: II

The morning after Woe-
'Tis frequently the Way-
Surpasses all that rose before-
For utter Jubilee-

Emily Dickinson

Barry showed up bright and early at the hospital like he promised. Told me about Snake's arrest. Told me Old Snake had a hissy-fit when the police arrived. Said Sheriff Jackson wasn't any too gentle on Snake. Think it was the first news that made me smile since Ma disappeared.

I told Barry my plans to leave the hospital and search for clues about Ma while Snake was still in jail. He didn't want me to leave the hospital without a doctor's say so. But I know grown-up rules. They wouldn't let me out without an adult. Sure din't want that adult to be Snake. And there wasn't anyone else. Afraid if I stayed, Social Services would be tryin' to find me a foster home. Wasn't waitin' around for that. And I wasn't gonna let Snake get out and destroy whatever evidence there was to find. Couldn't wait for no doctors. Couldn't wait for no Sheriff to get a search warrant.

Barry rode me to my house on the handlebars of his bike. Every bump in the road jolted my achin' brain. But I can handle pain. That's one lesson Snake taught me real good. I found some shovels in the basement, and we started diggin' in Ma's rose garden. My throat was dry. My head was poundin', but I wasn't gonna stop 'til I knew what happened to Ma. My shovel hit somethin' and I fell to my knees. The jolt through my head left me dizzy. The pain in my gut was worse. Shoved the dirt away with my bare hands. I had to know what was there, and I was terrified to find out at the same time. Pulled out Ma's violin case. Hugged it like it was a baby. Closest I been to Ma in seven years. Relieved it warn't her body. But horrified just the same. I knew she din't leave that violin behind. I knew for sure Snake had done somethin' to her, and I had to know what. Started digging again. Barry's shovel clanked against an object. We dropped to our knees and started clearin' the dirt away. This was somethin' big. Pulled out Ma's old suitcase. She used to call it "the coffin." I was scared it really was one. Head beatin' like a base drum. Stomach so knotted I thought I might puke. Opened it and near fainted with relief when it just had Ma's clothes. Pulled out her favorite white dress. Closed my eyes and inhaled, hoping to catch a whiff of Ma's scent. But it just smelled like dirt. Still I could picture her in it, shock of red hair pulled back in a headband. Wanted to cry. Wanted to scream. Din't do neither. Just knelt on the ground with that dress in my arms, lost in memories. Barry pulled me out of it.

"The sheds! Snake was coming from the sheds when the police came. And he freaked when he saw the cops. We have to get into those sheds."

I went for Snake's tools in the basement. Lock pick set, hammer, metal cutters. One way or another I was gettin' into those sheds. Learned more from Snake than I thought. Usin' the lock pick set, I had the locks open in no time. Opened the door. If my head hadn't been thunderin', I'da remembered this was the moonshine shed. Ran to the other one, head poundin' in time with each step. Awful stink comin' from the shed. Gut tellin' me this was it. Just got the chains off, when the Sheriff roared into the yard, sirens blarin'. Noise made me nauseous with pain, or I never woulda stopped. He had the deputy take us away to the police car. I was mad. I was so close, so close. Whatever was in there, I wanted to be the one who found out. Deputy was a big old broad. Couldn't see around her. But I heard. The sheriff had his walkie talkie on, and I heard him talking to someone.

"You're safe." Heard an ungodly howl of fear.

"I have to stay. He'll kill Tommy if I leave." Buried my head in my hands. That din't sound like Ma. Sounded like a wounded animal. Like a wounded animal guardin' her cub. So many thoughts bangin' around in my poor achin' head, it felt like it might explode. She was alive. My Ma was alive. She loved me. She'd been a prisoner in that hell-hole for seven years just to protect me. Heard the Sheriff cryin', sayin' somethin' 'bout her lookin' like someone from Buchenwald. I seen those war pictures. Couldn't envision Ma like that. Hairless skeletons they were. Not my Ma. She was beautiful, with that red-gold hair of hers. I wanted to see. Deputy made sure I couldn't. Heard Ma say,

"Don't want Tommy to see me like this." All this time, and she din't want me to see her. Deputy pulled away to make sure I wouldn't. But I looked at Barry. His eyes were wide with horror. Din't say a word. Din't have to. He'd seen.

Back to the Hospital: I

O the mother's joys!
The watching, the endurance, the precious love, the anguish,
The patiently yielded life.
    A Song of Joys from **Leaves of Grass** *by Walt Whitman*

The deputy took us into the hospital. The dispatcher must have called my mom. She was in the waiting room when we arrived. She put her arms around Tommy.

"I hear you found her, yourself."

"Yeah, but the Sheriff wouldn't let me go in to get her. After all this time, he wouldn't let me see her."

"Tommy I can only imagine how hard that was for you, but you've waited this long. Try to be patient just a little longer. I'm speaking as a mother here, when I tell you, she wouldn't want you to see her the way she was in that shed. Give the doctor time to examine her, and the nurse time to clean her up and get her settled. It would break her heart if she saw horror in your eyes when you saw her for the first time."

I tried to distract Tommy with talk. He wanted to ask me a couple of questions. I kind of knew what one would be.

"Will you tell me what happened to your hair?"

"Yeah. Now that we're brother bulb-heads, I guess I can tell you. Doc says I have something called Alopecia which causes hair loss. He doesn't know why I got it, and he doesn't know if my hair will grow back. The Doc says it's caused by my immune system making a mistake. The white blood cells are supposed to attack invaders like viruses and bacteria, but my white cells, are attacking my hair follicles, too. Well at least I know I've got some mean fighting white cells in case I ever get sick!"

"Rotten luck! I'm sorry I kidded you." Pointing to his bandaged head he asked, "Think God punished me with this because I teased you?"

"Nah. I don't believe God works that way. Besides, your hair will grow back. So what's your other question?"

"What the heck did you do to Weasel when he grabbed you? That was the coolest move I ever saw. You doubled him right over."

"It's called a roundhouse kick. I learned it in karate class."

"You take karate? Can you break boards and stuff?"

"Uh huh! I have a brown belt; that's right under black belt."

"So why didn't you use it on me when I was teasing you?"

"I wanted to. Boy did I want to. I almost did that one day."

"I know just what day you're talkin' about. I saw your whole body change. Your hands did somethin' funny. And your eyes were just starin' into mine. You din't seemed scared. You just seemed stone cold. So how come you didn't kick my ass? In your shoes, I would have."

"Because karate is for defense, not for offense. If I hit you first and my karate teacher found out about it, he would have thrown me out of class. But just count your lucky stars you didn't take the first swing."

"Yeah. Well, I have good instincts for survival. I din't know what was goin' on with you, but I sensed danger. That's why I backed off. And I don't back down often!" Our conversation came to a screeching halt when the nurse walked in to the room. She approached Tommy.

"The doctor has your mom on intravenous. She is very under-nourished and dehydrated. But she is a strong woman. It is sheer will that kept her alive. We bathed her and found her a turban for her head. She was only worried about looking pretty when she sees you. You have to be prepared for how thin she is. The hospital gown nearly fell off her, so we brought her a child's gown. We took turns spoon-feeding her soup and tea and crackers. Perhaps you can do that, too, when you go in to see her. But we don't want too eat too much at one time. Her stomach couldn't handle it. She's very anxious to see you. Go ahead, you can go in, Son."

Tommy was actually shaking. I walked down the hall with him. Tommy opened the door. I stopped in the doorway. I was an intruder, I knew, but I had to see her again. She was thin, very thin. But the nurses had put a little color on her cheeks, and the nightgown and turban helped. She no longer looked like the living corpse I had viewed in the shed. For Tommy's sake, I was glad. Tommy grabbed onto the door. For a minute, I thought he might faint. Then he took a deep breath and walked in.

"Oh God, Mama. What did he do to you?" Tears ran down Tommy's face. He started towards her as if to hug her. But he stopped short. I knew why. She looked so frail; she looked like she would break. Instead, he pulled a chair next to her bed next to her, and lay his bandaged head in her lap.

"What happened to you, Son? Did he do that?"

"No Ma. Weasel and Killer kidnapped me. I hit my head. The doctor had to shave part of my head to put in the stitches. I just have a little concussion, but I'll be fine." His mother smiled weakly, pushing the turban back enough for him to see her part of her red peach fuzz. Tommy blanched.

"Mama, your beautiful, long, red hair!

"It'll grow back. So will yours. Aren't the two of us a pair?"

I backed away from the doorway. I had seen enough. Too much. The two of them needed to be alone. Then I did something I hadn't done in a long time. I strode to the waiting room and hugged my mother.

Back to the Hospital: II

I can wade Grief-
Whole pools of it-
I'm used to that-
But the least push of Joy
Breaks up my feet-
And I tip-drunken—

Emily Dickinson

The deputy took us into the hospital. The dispatcher must have called Barry's mom. She was in the waiting room when we arrived. She hugged me. It felt safe, and I hadn't felt safe in a long time. I wanted to stay there. I wanted to cry. But I didn't, of course. I pulled back as she spoke to me.

"I'm so happy for you. I hear you found her yourself."

"Yeah, but the Sheriff wouldn't let me go in to get her. After all this time, he wouldn't let me see her."

"Tommy I can only imagine how hard that was for you, but you've waited this long. Try to be patient just a little longer. I'm speaking as a mother here, when I tell you, she wouldn't want you to see her the way she was in that shed. Give the doctor time to examine her, and the nurse time to clean her up and get her settled. It would break her heart if she saw horror in your eyes when you saw her for the first time."

I guess that adult logic made sense to her and my ma, but not to me. That was my Ma. I woun'ta felt horror when I saw her, no matter what she looked like. I shoulda been the one to save her. I shoulda been allowed to see her. I waited for what seemed like hours. Barry tried to get me talking. I knew he was trying to distract me, so I wouldn't keep looking at the clock. I figured it was a good time to ask him a few questions that had been bothering me. Found out he has Alopecia; that's what made him bald. Found out that he takes karate, and he breaks boards and everything. That's how he escaped from old Weasel. Sure was a good thing I din't fight him that day at school when he told me he wouldn't do my report for me. Finally, the nurse came in to speak to me.

"The doctor has your mother on intravenous. She is very under-nourished and dehydrated. But she is a strong woman. It is sheer will that kept her alive; sheer will and love for you. We bathed her and found her a turban for her head. She was only worried about looking pretty when she sees you. You have to be prepared for how thin she is. The hospital gown nearly fell off her, so we brought her a child's gown. We took turns spoon-feeding her soup and tea and crackers. Perhaps you can do that too when you go in to see her. But we don't want her to eat too much at one time. Her stomach couldn't handle it. She's very anxious to see you. Go ahead, you can go in, Son. But don't let her see how shocked you are at her appearance."

Time jumbled as I walked down the hall. I had to see her for myself for it to be real that Ma was alive. But I was afraid of what I'd see. I stumbled at the door. Had to grab onto it for support. Thought I might pass out, and it wasn't just from the pain in my head. I stood at the door, and took a deep breath. I opened the door.

"Oh God, Momma, what did he do to you?" Tears streaked down my face. Didn't care who saw. She was so thin, so thin. Wanted to run to her. Afraid to touch her. Looked like she might break. Pulled a chair next to her bed, and just lay there with my head in her lap. She stroked my bandaged head, tears running down her face.

"What happened to you, Son? Did he do that?" Here she was after seven years in hell, worrying about me. I could feel the pent up years of love and worry in her voice. The tears kept flowing. Mine and hers. Neither of us had someone love us in seven years. At last I was able to answer her.

"No Ma. Snake didn't do this. Weasel and Killer kidnapped me. I hit my head. The doctor had to shave part of my head to put in the stitches. I just have a little concussion, but I'll be fine." Ma smiled weakly, pushing the turban back enough for me to see part of her peach fuzz hair.

"He made me do that," she whispered. I gasped!

"Mama, your beautiful, long, red hair!"

"It'll grow back. So will yours. Aren't the two of us a pair?"

"We sure are. I love you Mama."

"I love you too, Tommyboy." Tommyboy! Mama's nickname for me. Nobody'd called me that in a month of Sundays. It sure sounded good. A nurse came in. I thought she was going to try to make me leave, and I was fixin' for a fight. Instead she said,

"Boy, what were you thinking leaving the hospital this morning before the doctor checked you out? We have readmitted you for further observation. No telling what damage you did to yourself with your escapades today. We don't usually put men and women in the same room, but Doc says under the circumstances, it's all right if we give you the other bed in this room. But stay put!"

"Yes, Ma'am. Thank you, Ma'am. And don't worry about me leavin'. You coun't chase me loose from this room with a stick of dynamite." Ma and I talked and talked. She asked about school. I told her about the class project that Barry and I were working on. I told her about Miss Jenkins and the writing book.

"Would you let me see your writing?" I hesitated. What if she thought it was stupid? Barry had brought my book bag to the hospital. I looked to see if the writin' book was even in there. It was. I took a deep breath and showed her. She smiled at what she read.

"I'm proud of you, Son. These are good." She pointed to one song lyric. "I'd love a copy of this one. I'd like to set it to music." She didn't think it was sissy writin'. We could have talked longer, but the nurse came back. She had a pain pill for me. It's strange. During the whole conversation with Ma, I don't remember my head hurtin'. But as soon as the nurse came in, it started thunderin' again. But I still said,

"I don't want that. It makes me sleepy, and Ma and me have a lot of catchin' up to do." But the nurse whispered to me,

"Your Ma needs her rest. If you go to bed, maybe we can get her to sleep, too." I took the pill.

My Friends: I

"A friend in need is a friend indeed."

English Proverb

The whole school knew what happened. It was in the local newspapers. Out of state newspapers even picked up the story. It made the t.v. news. Everyone was calling me a hero. All the boys who had ignored me when Tommy told them to, now wanted to be friends. Girls who would never have looked at me wanted to stand next to me in line. April Baker, the prettiest girl in school, approached me. She was one of the many who'd called me Barry the Bulb-head.

"Do you want to take me to the New Year's Dance?"

"Thank you, but I already have a date."

"With who?"

"Rebecca Jackson."

"Well, you can break it."

"No, I couldn't do that."

"You can't tell me you would rather take her to the dance than me." The arrogance in her voice annoyed me.

"Actually, yes, I would!" Boy the look of surprise on her face when I turned her down was priceless! Rebecca was nearby trying to pretend she wasn't listening. I walked over and took her hand. Her face had that mousy, timid expression, I hadn't seen on it for a while.

"I'd understand if you'd rather go with her. She's the most popular girl in school."

"Yes. But you're the nicest. I meant it when I said I'd rather go with you."

She removed her glasses to wipe them. Her big brown eyes were sparkling. The mousy, timid expression had been replaced with an ear-to-ear smile that lit up her face. It dawned on me that we were alike. I was glad. A minute later, Ted came up to me.

"Is it true you turned down April Baker? Are you crazy?"

"Yes! I turned her down. And no, I'm not crazy! She's not my friend. She isn't interested in me. She's interested in dating Barry Brenner, the hero, because she might get her picture in the paper if she's seen with me."

"Who care's why she wanted to go with you? She's April Baker!"

"I care. I like Rebecca. My mother told me you find out who your friends are when things are tough. Rebecca was my friend when no one else was." Ted had the good grace to lower his eyes when I said that. "And she'll still be my friend when this hero thing is over."

My Friends: II

If at the end... I have lost every other friend on earth, I shall have at least one friend left...

Abraham Lincoln

Barry came by again today. He told me about April Baker asking him to the Holiday Dance.

"I hope you told her to drop dead. That girl treats me like something she wants to wipe off the bottom of her shoes. And more than once I heard her and her other cheerleader friends laughing at you."

"I did better than that. I told her I already had a date, and I much preferred to go with Becky. You should have seen the expression on April's face! And Becky had a grin from ear to ear."

"I never thought much about Rebecca. Thought she was a bit of a mouse. But she's different when she's with you. That girl is surely sweet on you."

"I kind of like her, too. When you were teasing me, and the others joined in, she stood by me."

"Sorry 'bout that."

"I know. And I learned who my real friends are. And strangely enough, you seem to be one of them."

"Just so you know, if I get it wrong sometimes, I haven't had much practice being a friend. You're about the only friend I ever had in New Hope. So if I screw it up again, like I did the last time I teased you, call me on it."

"Oh, you can just bet I will."

"Did I tell you about all the reporters around, wanting Mama and me to tell them our stories? One even sneaked into the room wearing a doctor's jacket and snapped our picture. I thought Mama was like to die. Everyone in the state must know about you and me and the bank robbers, and Mama in the shed. Poor Mama is so embarrassed. She was always warning me not to air our dirty laundry in public."

"I'm afraid it's worse than that. The national news picked up the story. Everyone in the country is asking questions. The press has been hounding me. I told them a little about the robbery and the cave, but I wouldn't tell them anything about you or your Mama. Told them they'd have to ask you."

"Thanks for that."

"No problem. But the others in school aren't as respectful of your privacy. To hear her tell it, April and you are lifelong friends. And Ted may be your new best buddy. Just about everyone at school is talking. And if they don't know the facts, that still doesn't stop them from blabbing."

"Nothin' I can do about it. Put a camera in front of some people, and their fool mouths don't stop running. If people want to think the worst of me, I can live with it. They always have, and most of the time they were right. But if I hear anyone badmouthin' Mama, then they'll be some fireworks."

"I didn't hear anyone saying anything bad about your mother. And the sheriff has a man outside the building. If any press people try to sneak in again, they'll be arrested. By the way, where is your Ma?"

"She's having some tests done. She should be back soon."

"Well, I'd best be going. Tonight is a karate night. Oh, I almost forgot. Miss Jenkins sent some homework for you. She said, 'No hurry. Work on it when you feel up to it.' And the class made you this card. Everyone signed it. My Ma said to tell yours that she'll be up tomorrow, and to give a call if you or she need us to bring anything."

"Thanks. See ya."

"See ya."

The Visitors: I

"Happy he with such a mother! Faith in womankind beats with his blood."

The Princess *by Alfred, Lord Tennyson*

Ma and I were visiting Tommy and his mom when an older couple came to the door. They hesitated there, as if not sure they should enter. He was tall, graying. I don't know much about clothes, but I could tell theirs were expensive. She had dark red hair, sprinkled with grey. Their eyes were sad. The woman gasped when she saw Tommy's mom. Tommy and his mom looked up.

"Mama! Papa!" whispered Tommy's mom. Tears streamed down her face, down their faces, as they rushed to the bed to hug her.

"Mary Rose, my baby" the woman cried. When Mrs. Thompson finally regained some composure, she said,

"This is my son, Tommy."

"My grandson? I have a grandson!" The woman walked over to Tommy's bed, and took his face in her hands. She just looked at him for the longest time. Tears still flowed down her face.

"You have your mother's eyes. How old are you?"

"Fourteen, Ma'am." Her eyes widened. Mary Thompson gasped,

"Forgive my manners. This is my friend Molly Brenner and her son Barry. Barry is the one who saved Tommy and helped Tommy save me. My parents, Sean and Mary Beth O'Shea."

"Nice to meet you," my mother said.

"Glad to meet you, Ma'am, Sir," I said. Mr. O'Shea said,

"The pleasure is ours. Young man, I don't know how to thank you. I will be forever grateful. If there is ever anything I can do for you, all you have to do is ask."

"Thank you, Sir." My mother put her hand on my shoulder and gently pushed me toward the door as she spoke.

"You have a lot of catching up to do. You should be alone. We'll stop by tomorrow. It was very nice to meet you."

THE VISITORS: II

"O to go back to the place where I was born…"
A Song of Joys from **Leaves of Grass** *by Walt Whitman*

Barry and his Ma came by again. I noticed Barry glance at the doorway, so I looked over. Two people stood there. Her red hair was a faded version of Ma's. He was tall. He wore a suit, so I knew he wasn't from around here. He looked distinguished, important. Maybe it was the way he carried himself, tall and straight. The Mayor! I knew it was the Mayor, Ma's dad. Yet they both seemed afraid at the doorway. Ma looked up, pale like she'd seen a ghost, and whispered,

"Mama! Papa!"

The woman cried "Mary Rose." For a minute I think they all forgot that anyone else was in the room. Then Ma remembered I was there.

"This is my son, Tommy." I watched their faces carefully. Would they be glad? Sorry? The woman's jaw dropped.

"I have a grandson?" She walked over to me and lifted my chin with one hand. It was a gentle touch, like Ma's. She stared into my face.

"You have your mother's eyes. How old are you?"

"Fourteen, Ma'am." Her eyes widened. I knew she understood why Ma had married Snake, why Ma had run away. The moment was awkward, made more so by Ma's sudden realization that Barry and his Ma were still in the room. After quick introductions, Barry and his Ma beat a hasty exit.

"Mary Rose, why didn't you tell us about the boy?"

"I did, Mama. I wrote you a letter when he was born. You never answered it. I figured you were ashamed of us."

"We never got a letter. We tried to call you a few weeks after you left. John answered the phone. He said you didn't want to talk to us. We wrote you letters asking you to come home or at least contact us. We never heard from you."

It occurred to me that I didn't even know Snake's real name was John. Nobody in New Hope ever called him that. Ma was angry.

"Snake! That snake! I never got any letters. He never told me you called. In fact, he told me he called you, because he knew how upset I was, and you told him, 'She made her bed. She'll have to lie in it.' He said you accused him of being a thief who took advantage of my innocence and stole their child, which by the way, was the truth. He always made it clear that I had to stay with him. He told me I had no where else to go, because I didn't have any money, and you didn't want me."

"Oh honey, I know we said some terrible things to you when you came back after eloping with John. But our hearts were broken. You were our only child. Your bright future, your music, were gone. And you didn't even seem happy. That was the worst of it. We didn't understand. But as soon as we calmed down some, we tried to reach you. And John blocked us at every turn. It never dawned on us that he had never told you that we called. We just figured you couldn't forgive us for the mean things we said."

"Mama, I was never angry at you. I was ashamed. I couldn't stay in O'Shea. Papa was Mayor. What would the townspeople have said? They'd count the days. They'd know the baby was born too soon. I couldn't shame you that way. I couldn't tell you what really happened. Snake said no one would believe me. It would be my word against his. And he said if I told anyone, he'd never marry me, and neither would anyone else, and the baby would be a b…." She didn't finish. She looked in horror at me. I think she'd forgotten again that I was there.

"Tommy, I'm sorry, baby. I didn't want you to hear that." It all made sense. Why she'd married a snake like Snake. He'd forced her. She hadn't wanted me at all. I was the reason she had been trapped into her horrible life. I was the reason she left O'Shea. The reason she had never been a concert pianist. The dirty secret she was ashamed even to tell her parents. No wonder I was always in trouble. I was the son of a thief, a wife-beater, a rapist. And like Miss Walker always said, "The apple doesn't fall far from the tree."

"I'm sorry, Mama."

"For what? None of this is your fault. You're not responsible for Snake's actions."

"But how can you not think of what he did every time you look at me? How can you not see the family, the home, the career you gave up because of me? If I were you, I'd hate me. I'm his son. Suppose I turn out just like him. I've done some pretty bad things in my life."

"You're my son. That's what I see when I look at you. My son! My one reason for living. From the moment I first held you in my arms, I knew you were my miracle, my joy. Yes, you have his genes. But you have mine, too. You get to choose whose life you want to copy. I've heard you play the piano. You've shown me those wonderful poems and songs you write. You could never be like him. As for doing some bad things, you didn't have me there to teach you right from wrong. You only had him for an example. From now on, I'll be with you every step of the way."

"Mary Rose, what are you going to do now?"

"I don't know, Mama. I can't go back to that awful house again. But I don't have any money to move."

"But you do! Did you forget that Grampa left you an inheritance that was to come to you when you turned 25? You have 25 thousand dollars, plus interest."

"Oh my God! I did forget. When I was twenty-five, I was Snake's prisoner. I was just thinking about surviving." After thinking for a minute, she added, "Then I can buy a house. I can get Tommy and me some decent clothes."

"You can do that, although your father and I would like to buy both of you some things, if you'll let us. And… would you consider moving back to O'Shea? We have 14 years to catch up on with you and our grandson. It would be wonderful to have you near us again. You're all the family we have." Mama looked at me.

"I have to talk to Tommy before I make a decision like that. This town hasn't been a happy place for either of us, but there are some wonderful people here who have been good friends to us. I'd hate to leave them. And Tommy is just finishing up eighth grade. I don't want to pull him out of school now. He has a teacher he really likes this year. Next year he'll be starting high school. When he's moving to a new school anyway, that would be a better time for us to move. It's hard to make new friends in the middle of a school year."

"Well, at least come home for winter vacation. You know what a fuss the town makes over Christmas. Then maybe we'll rent a place here for a few months. Papa is retired now as Mayor. He still owns the business, but others mostly run it. We could be away for awhile." She looked at her husband, her eyebrows raised. He nodded.

"I'd love to go home for Christmas. Tommy has never had a proper O'Shea Christmas. I think it's about time he did.   And I'd love to see the town again. It was the last place I was truly happy. I want Tommy to experience what I had there. And if he likes it, maybe at the end of the school year, we'll move back."

My life was changing awful fast. We weren't poor any more. I could have new clothes like everyone else. I could have a nice place to live. I didn't have many happy memories of life in New Hope, but I wasn't sure I wanted to move, either. I finally had a friend. I finally had a teacher who thought I was smart. But Mama. Mama'd been through so much. If being in O'Shea would make her happy, I couldn't say no. I know how much I missed Mama when she was gone. Maybe she'd missed her parents just as much. It might be nice to have grandparents, as long as they don't try to boss me around.

CHRISTMAS 1962: I

"My best of wishes for your merry Christmases and your happy New Years, your long lives and your true prosperities."
Doctor Marigold's Prescriptions *by Charles Dickens*

Christmas Eve was always a big deal in New Hope. Since I was still considered a hero, I got to light the town tree that night. The mayor shook my hand. The sheriff was on hand with his wife and Becky. She beamed when I asked her to stand next to me with my Ma and Pa when I lit the tree. Mayor Kolter gave me a key to the city, and Sheriff Jackson gave me an honorary sheriff's badge. Then I pulled the switch and the tree lit up the whole town square. It was really neat!

Afterwards, Becky and Ted and I went caroling with a group from our class. I knew Becky sang with her Girl Scout Troop, but I was still surprised at what a great voice she had. I sounded like a croaking toad, but no one seemed to care. Mrs. Jackson asked us in to warm up. On the table was an elaborate gingerbread house decorated with M&M's and white icing. She told us Becky had helped her make it. It was so nice, it seemed a shame to eat it, but we did! Then we washed it down with apple cider.

Later, we all went to church, and I didn't mind because we were allowed to wear our Christmas stocking caps in church that night. Becky was in the choir. She sang a solo of *Silent Night.* Wow! She can really sing. I was proud when she looked right at me while she was singing. My favorite part of the service was the nativity story, with songs and live animals in the nativity scene. It was pretty funny when one of the sheep took a dump on the stage right in the middle of everything.

Then we went home. Ma and Pa and I hung our stockings. We set up the train around our tree. Most of the tree was already decorated, but as always, we put on the finishing touches that night. We strung popcorn. We hung some candy canes on the branches. Then Ma brought out the last of the ornaments-the special ones. The little lopsided clay gingerbread boy, I made in Sunday school when I was five. The little wooden baby boy with BARRY on it that dad had carved for my first Christmas. The popsicle-stick star with glitter on it that Ma helped me make when I was two. I know it's corny, but I loved those ornaments.

Finally we set out a dish of cookies and milk. I was way too old to believe in Santa Claus, but it was tradition. I was so excited I was sure I wouldn't sleep, but I did.

I awoke early. My stocking was filled with a yoyo, a bag of marbles, and five packs of baseball cards, plus some candy. I bought Pa some tools and a new fishing rod. For Ma I got a sweater and a pocketbook that Pa had helped me pick out. But their eyes really lit up when I gave them the gift that hadn't cost me anything. I'd found an old copy of their wedding picture. I made a sketch of it and framed it for them. The way they fussed, you'd have thought I gave them a Picasso.

Pa got me a new fishing rod-I guess we think alike! Ma got me an art kit with charcoals and watercolors and color pencils and sketch pads. It was great! Then I got a snorkel, mask and fins. Pa said that gift was for the family gift, the trip to Florida he had been talking about earlier in the year. Pa said,

"I added one more stop to the trip just for you. I just found out about a new underwater park called Pennekamp that recently opened in Key Largo. It has beautiful fish and great coral reefs. It is one of the best snorkeling and scuba sites in Florida. As soon as I heard about this place, I knew you would love it. We are booked to leave in June, just a few days after your graduation. What do you think?"

It has been a long time since I hugged my Pa. I'm getting too old for that. We usually do the handshake thing now. But this time I made an exception. I'm going snorkeling in an underwater park. I didn't even know there was such a thing. I can't wait until June!

After breakfast, I walked over to Becky's. The sweater sets, skirts, and knee-hi socks she wore to school hid her figure. But today she was in a shirt-waist dress, stockings, and low heels. They really showed off her shape, and her legs. A tiny waist, easy for me to slip my arm around, if I got the nerve to try. And when had she developed to fill out the dress top so well? And legs that didn't quit. Just looking at her gave me ideas that would get my face slapped. Not that I would try anything. Becky was a good girl. But I couldn't stop the image from swirling through my brain.

"Why are you staring? Do I have food stuck in my teeth or something?"

"Uh, uh. I'm sorry. I didn't mean to stare. I, uh, just never saw you in a dress and stockings. You really look nice." I knew my face was beet red. It was a good thing she couldn't read my thoughts.

She flushed with pleasure. "Thanks."

"I got you something."

Ma had said I couldn't get anything personal, so she helped me pick out a collectible doll, a beautiful Christmas caroler wearing glasses. I handed it to Becky.

"Thank you. I love it." Then, a little afraid she would think it hokey, I handed her a picture I had sketched of her. I'd put it in a picture frame. She smiled when she saw the doll; she beamed when she saw the picture.

"I love this. I'm going to hang it in my room. Do you really think I look like that?"

"Yes. That's exactly how you look to me."

"But that girl is pretty."

"Yes," I agreed, "she is." I moved towards her. This time when I kissed her there was no stupid Halloween costume in the way. It felt kind of nice. And I managed to slip my arms around her waist and pull her closer. Her cheeks were rosy when we moved apart.

"I hope you like my gifts for you. They're not as special as this painting, but I tried to do something just for you." She made me 6 gingerbread men. Each one had something different on it. One said BASEBALL BARRY. It was wearing a little baseball cap on its head and holding a bat. One said KARATE KING. That one had a brown belt around its waist. One said MY HERO and had a little police badge on its chest. The one wearing a graduation cap said STAR STUDENT. The one that said FISHING FIEND was carrying a fishing rod. And the last one, AMAZING ARTIST, was holding a little palette.

"These are fantastic. I almost wish they were ceramic, so I could keep them. They are too nice to eat." She gave me one of those ear-to-ear smiles of hers, that always made my heart beat faster, and after the kiss and hug, it was already doing double-time.

"I spent all night making them. Do you really like them?" I nodded. Then she gave me a set of colored pens to use for my art.

"These are great! That's the only art supply that I needed that wasn't in the art kit my Ma got me." Her parents came into the room.

"Mom, Dad, look what Barry made for me." She held up the sketch. Her mother looked at it for a long time, as if examining every detail.

"Barry, this is really phenomenal. It doesn't just capture her pretty features. Somehow you've also caught her gentle spirit. You are very talented."

"Thank you, Ma'am. I was trying to draw a picture to show Becky how I see her. Sometimes I think she doesn't know that she is special."

"You are very perceptive and mature. I'm glad my daughter is going to the Holiday Dance with such a nice young man."

"Thank you, Ma'am." By then, Becky had me by my arm and was pulling me out of the room.

"Barry has to leave now, Mom. His family is waiting for him."

"Merry Christmas, Mr. and Mrs. Jackson."

"Merry Christmas, Barry, and send our regards to your parents." I was out the door.

"Why did you do that, Becky? Do you want me to leave?" It was then I realized how red her face was.

"No, I was just trying to get you away from my mother before I died of embarrassment."

"Why? She was just being nice. You pulled me out of there so fast, I left my presents behind."

"You wait here. I'll get them for you." I looked at my watch when she came out with my stuff.

"I guess I do have to go. We're having dinner tonight at my grandparents' house."

"I have to go in and help my mother set the table. My grandparents, and my aunt and uncle and cousins are all coming here."

"I'll see ya. Thanks for the presents. They're great." I thought about trying for another kiss, but just then her little sister came to the door. "Kissy, kissy," she teased.

"Mama," Becky wailed, "Will you get Karen out of here?"

"Karen, leave your sister alone! Come in here right now!" The mood had passed. The door was open and her mother was in the living room. I couldn't risk a kiss.

"Um, I'll pick you up at 8:00 next week for the New Year's dance. Is it all right if we walk? Then we can be alone. Otherwise my Pa will have to drive us."

"I'd rather walk. I'll see you. And I love my picture. Thank you, again."

When I got home, I showed Ma my stuff.

"I wish I could keep these gingerbread men. They're too nice to eat. I'd really like to hang them in my room."

"They really are cute," Ma agreed. Pa suggested shellacking them.

"We could try shellacking one. Then if it doesn't work, you can still eat the others. We can do it tomorrow. For today let's just put them in a plastic container. I don't want you to go to Grandma's smelling like shellac."

Christmas 1962: II

'Twas Christmas told the merriest tale.
Lochinvar *by Sir Walter Scott*

I never had a real Christmas before. Ma tried in the early years, but we never had much money. Snake had a bad habit of tyin' one on for Christmas Eve, and then he'd be rantin' and ravin' the next day, and we'd hafta tiptoe around. I cou'nt remember a Christmas he din't ruin. The last Christmas before Ma disappeared, she tried to make a real Christmas for me. It was hard 'cause Snake never gave her any money. She knew I wanted a bike, and she knew Snake would never spend the money for one. She did sewing for people to make extra money. She even did ironing. And she had to do it when Snake wasn't there cause he'd a been mad if he knew. She made a new outfit for me and one for Snake, too. Me and Ma went into the woods and cut down a small tree. We decorated it with strings of popcorn and paper chains. She bought a secondhand bike with her money and painted it up so it looked brand new. I was so proud of that bike. I thought it was the best Christmas ever.

Snake hadn't come home all night, but Ma fixed the two of us a special meal with ham and sweet potatoes and everything. I rode that bike around the yard all afternoon. When it got dark, I didn't want to leave it out in case it snowed. So I brought it into the living room. Later that night Snake came in drunk as a skunk. He staggered into the living room and bumped into the bike. It fell with a crash, and he fell with it. He let out a string of swear words, grabbed a hammer, and smashed my bike to smithereens. The noise woke me and Ma and we ran into the room. Ma tried to stop him, and he knocked her flat. I was cryin' and screamin', and he cuffed me good and called me "Sissy Boy" for cryin'. That was my last Christmas.

Now here I was in O'Shea, Virginia. Instead of being the poor white trash of New Hope, I was part of the wealthiest and most respected family in

O'Shea. At the Christmas parade Grandpa, as the former mayor, was Grand Marshall. I got to ride in a big white limousine with him at the front of the parade.

We stayed in Grandpa's house which was a mansion with big marble pillars in front, like something from a movie. There was a dining room with a table that must have sat fifty people! I had my own bedroom suite with a walk-in closet and my very own private bathroom. That bedroom was bigger than our whole house in New Hope! The Christmas tree was two stories high, covered with lights and crystal and china ornaments. It was bigger and fancier than the one in the town square. But we still made popcorn strings to decorate it. I got to lean over the second floor balcony to place the star on top.

Grandma didn't have to do other people's laundry and sewing to pay for gifts. In fact she had a housekeeper, a cook/ laundress, and a gardener working for her full-time. When I saw how Ma grew up, it made me mad to think how hard Snake made her work. The housekeeper cried when we walked in.

"Miss Mary, I never thought I'd lay eyes on you again. It near broke your Papa's heart when you left. You always was his princess." Ma nearly got lost in the big arms that enfolded her. "Dory, please, just call me Mary. This is my boy, Tommy." I got hugged till I thought I couldn't breathe.

"It sure is nice to have a young'un here again. I tended your Ma since she was knee high to a grasshopper."

There were so many presents under the tree, I didn't know what to open first on Christmas morning. I got shoes and sneakers, a new jacket, pants and shirts. I'll never be able to wear 'em all! I'm not sure I'll take to wearin' shoes, but it sure is nice to have a choice. I got a brand new fishing pole, a baseball glove that didn't come from someone's hand-me-downs, and a real English racer bike. I felt kinda like that boy Oliver in the book *Oliver Twist* we were readin' in school!

Half the town must have come for holiday dinner and everyone was fussin' over me and Ma. There was more food on that table in one night than Snake an' me had in a year. There was turkey and ham and stuffin' and mashed potatoes and yams and collard greens and pumpkin pies and apple pies and shoofly pie and cakes of every kind. And Dory kept loadin' my plate with everything. I coun't hardly move when I was done. Gran'pa O'Shea said,

"Boy you must have a hollow leg. I don't know where a skin- and-bones boy like you put all that food." Gran'ma O'Shea told me,

"You just keep eating like that, Tommyboy. You're a growing boy, and it does my heart good to see a young'un with a healthy appetite."

Happy New Year: I

"Now the New Year reviving old Desires"
The Rubaiyat of Omar Khayyam by   Edward Fitzgerald

Ma helped me tie my tie. Who invented this form of torture? I feel like I'm choking. And my feet are screaming about these dress shoes. Pa handed me a box as I walk out the door.

"Give these to Becky. You should bring a girl flowers when you take her to a dance."

"Thanks, Pa. I should have thought of that."

I walked over to Becky's house and knocked on her door. Her little sister opened the door.

"Becky" she shouted, "Your love is here."

"Mama, make Karen shut up."

"Karen, leave Becky alone. And Becky, don't say 'shut up.' It's not nice."

As Becky came down the steps I was nervously fumbling with the box in my hands.

"Come on in. Sorry about my sister. You're lucky you're an only child!"

"I don't know. I always wanted a little brother." I stopped fumbling with the flowers and looked up at her. Wow! The blue dress clung to curves, her Christmas dress had merely hinted at. Her hair had been released from the perpetual ponytail. And she wasn't wearing glasses.

"Wow! You look fabulous. Where are your glasses?"

"No more glasses! I got contact lenses for Christmas."

"You look amazing. I never saw you with your hair down before. I like it.

"Do you? It's called a page boy."

"Well they misnamed it. You definitely don't look like a boy!" Becky laughed.

"And that dress, wow! You look great in that color blue." I felt like an idiot saying "Wow!" again and again. But I really couldn't find any other words. My mind didn't seem to be working right. As I looked at her, there were feelings stirring in me that I'd never felt before. Exciting, scary feelings.

"Thanks. You look good, too. I never saw you in a suit before."

"Oh, I almost forgot. These are for you." I winced when I realized my voice had cracked. I handed her the flower box.

"Orchids! My favorite! That was really nice of you. Can you pin them on?" I took the flowers and pin out of the box. I moved toward her not quite sure what to do or where to put them. Suppose I stuck her with the pin.

"Here, just below my right shoulder would be good." My hands were shaking, and, as I reached toward her shoulder, I grazed her breast.

"Oh, my God. I'm sorry," I mumbled. And I was sorry, sort of. But those strange stirrings inside intensified. And for a moment the image of me touching her again, on purpose, flashed through my head. I didn't, of course, but I was terrified she'd be able to read what I was thinking.

"It's okay." But she was blushing. I was all thumbs. I finally got the darn thing pinned in place, but the corsage looked like it was ready to fall. I was silently cursing my Pa for suggesting the flowers, and my own body for betraying me.

"We'd better go," I croaked. She seemed so mature, so self-assured, so un-Becky-like, but in the best possible way.

"Okay, but I have to wait for my mom to come down." She called upstairs, "Mom, we're ready to leave."

"Be right there, Sweetie." She came down in a dressy black dress with a camera in hand.

"Don't you look nice, Barry."

"Thank you, Ma'am."

"Look, Mom, Barry bought me orchids."

"Very nice." She straightened the orchids on Becky's shoulder.

"Stand by the door. I want to get a picture of you going to your first big dance." Becky winced at her Mom's words, but then we dutifully smiled for the camera. We posed until I saw spots before my eyes.

"Okay, enough, Mom. We want to leave."

"If you want to wait a few minutes, we'll drive you. We are just waiting for the babysitter. Your dad and I are chaperones, you know." I saw Becky's face fall.

"Great!" she muttered under her breath.

"My parents are chaperones, too," I whispered.

"Thanks for offering to take us, but we'd really like to walk," Becky chimed in.

"Okay. Then wear your coat. It's chilly."

"But it will crush my flower!"

"Okay then, take my cape." I helped her on with the cape and we escaped out the door. Fortunately, it was only a three block walk to the school. The gym was decorated with balloons and crepe paper. The Christmas tree and lights were still up, but there were also hats and blowers on the table for New Year's Eve. Most of the students were there. Many had come alone. A lot of the parents were there as chaperones. Miss Jenkins was there with Mr. Faulkner, the gym teacher.

"Look," Becky whispered. "They're holding hands!" I turned to Ted, forgetting that I was still annoyed at him.

'Look! Mr. Faulkner and Miss Jenkins are holding hands." Becky nudged Cheryl and pointed.

"What's everybody whisperin' about?" I looked to see who was talking. The voice sounded familiar, but I never would have recognized Tommy in his new suit, tie, dress shoes, and hair combed so that the stitches were hardly visible.

"Hey, I didn't know you were coming. When did you get back?"

"Today. My Mama didn't want me to miss the dance. I told her I wouldn't mind missing it at all. I can't dance, which is just as well because nobody will dance with me anyhow. But Mama insisted. She's coming to chaperone. And she'll play the piano when the D.J. takes a break."

I put my arm around Becky. Tommy's eyes widened when he saw her.

"You look very nice, Rebecca."

"What? You actually know my name? I thought you only called me Metal Mouth or Four-eyed Mouse." Becky's tone was teasing, not angry, but Tommy apologized anyway.

"Sorry, about that. I was a real jerk. But you are certainly no Metal Mouth or Four-eyed Mouse tonight!" Turning to me, he joked, "It's a good thing we're friends or I might go after your girl." Tightening my grip on Becky's waist, I joked back.

"Just remember, I know karate, and some things are worth fighting for."

April came over, with her over-made up eyes and lips, smiling her big fake smile, and insinuated herself all over Tommy.

"Looking good, Tommy. Do you want to dance with me?" Tommy disengaged himself. He actually looked physically nauseous at her touch.

"Sorry April. I was just about to dance with Cheryl." Cheryl looked surprised when Tommy reached for her hand, but she played along. April's eyes flashed in anger and she stalked away.

"Thanks for playin' along, Cheryl. I can't stand that girl. She treated me like dog sh…uh… dirt for the last eight years, and suddenly she's my best friend. You don't hafta dance with me if you don't want to. I'm not much of a dancer."

"It's a slow dance. You don't have to know how to dance. You just stand close and rock back and forth. Come on, I'll show you." Tommy and Cheryl headed for the dance floor. I held my hand out for Becky, and we followed them. Becky smiled that breath-stopping smile of hers.

"It's our first dance together, and I love this song." I listened. It was Elvis, singing "I Can't Help Falling in Love With You."

"I like this one, too."

"Could we make it our song?"

"Okay." We danced a little closer. I liked my arms around her. Ma appeared out of nowhere with her camera, and snapped a picture of us. I know my face flushed, and I eased my hold on Becky's waist. Honestly, sometimes my Ma can be so embarrassing! As the night went on, we all sang along to Brenda Lee singing "Rockin' Around the Christmas Tree." We danced in the twist contest to "The Peppermint Twist" and "Let's Twist Again." We didn't come close to winning the contest, but it was fun. Becky was a good dancer, but I wasn't much of a partner. She didn't seem to mind. April made a spectacle of herself with her x-rated version of the twist. Mr. Stimson, approached, whispered something to her, and she stalked off the floor. The rest of us laughed. When the song "He's a Rebel" came on, Tommy joked,

"That should have been my theme song!" Next, the disc jockey played "Bobby's Girl." Becky sang it to me in that amazing voice of hers, but she changed the words to "I want to be Barry's Girl." I thought my buttons would pop! We came to the countdown before midnight. I pulled Becky towards the hallway. I didn't want to be in the middle of a crowd for the big kiss. 5…4…3…2…1… Happy New Year! I kissed her. Not the little pecks we'd exchanged so far. A real kiss, the kind that got my insides churning again. She was breathless.

"Happy New Year, Barry."

"Happy New Year, Becky."

A moment later, we sensed that we were not alone. Another couple had edged into the hallway for privacy: Miss Jenkins and Mr. Faulkner. Their kiss was definitely not the just-friends kind. Becky and I scooted back into the gym before they noticed us. Becky whispered,

"I'll bet she won't be Miss Jenkins, by next year." It made me kind of uncomfortable seeing teachers like that. I mean I guess I knew that they were human, but I didn't want to think of them doing stuff like going to the john or kissing someone. We joined the group in singing "Auld Lang Syne", although I never could figure out what that meant. And then too soon, the last record went on, "The Party's Over."

Tommy asked to walk Cheryl home. I walked Becky home. It was a cold, crisp, star-filled night. I was feeling bold. I put my arm around her. She didn't resist. In fact, for just a second, she rested her head on my shoulder. We stopped to kiss three times along the way. All in all, it was a great start to the New Year.

Happy New Year: II

Will you, won't you, will you,
Won't you, will you join the dance.
From Alice's Adventures in Wonderland *by Lewis Carroll*

We came back from Grandma and Grandpa's just in time for New Year's. Mama wanted me to go to the New Year's Dance. I told her I didn't want to go. But I think she was looking forward to a night out as well, and she had volunteered to be one of the chaperones. I let her convince me, although I knew I'd stand in a corner alone all night. After a lifetime in torn pants and worn out sneaks, when I wore shoes at all, I can't say I loved the feel of a suit and tie and shoes, but anything for Mama. And before we left O'Shea, Grandpa paid his barber a small fortune to style my hair so that the stitches hardly showed.

When we got to the dance, Mama said she wanted to stop at the lady's room to check her makeup. I think she just knew that I would feel awkward walkin' in with my Mama. So I went in alone. I saw Barry and Rebecca and Cheryl and Ted and some others in a group, whisperin'. I walked over.

"What's goin' on?" When Barry turned around, for a minute he had this blank look on his face. His eyes became saucers when he realized it was me! We talked a little, and then Rebecca joined us. Boy has that ugly duckling become a swan!

"You look nice, Rebecca," I told her. She made some comment about being surprised I knew her name since I always called her Metal Mouth or Four-eyed Mouse. I could tell from her tone she wasn't angry, but I apologized anyway.

"Sorry about that. But you are certainly no Metal Mouth or Four Eyed Mouse tonight!" I turned to Barry.

"It's a good thing we are friends or I might go after your girl." He returned the banter.

"Don't forget I know karate and some things are worth fighting for." He was joking, but the way his arm tightened around her waist, I knew he meant it. Of course, the way she was lookin' at him, I knew I wouldn't stand a chance anyway. Again that regret ached inside me, that no girl looked at me that way. Just then April came after and wrapped herself around me askin' me if I want to dance. I had to admit the girl had a body that wouldn't quit. Too bad her bust size was higher than her I.Q. But I actually felt physically sick from her touch as I tried to control my temper. That girl had taunted me, treated me like pond scum from the day she met me. Now that I was somebody from a family with money, she was my friend. I mighta banged her if the chance arose, but I sure din't wanna dance with her. I removed her hands and backed away, repulsed by her touch. I wanted a girlfriend, but I wasn't that desperate.

"I was just about to dance with Cheryl." I blurted. I reached for Cheryl's hand, and thankfully, she took it. April stalked off. I let go of Cheryl's hand.

"Thanks for playin' along. I can't stand that girl. She treated me like sh… dog dirt for the last eight years, and suddenly she's my best friend. You don't hafta dance with me if you don't want to. I really can't dance."

I thought, Man, I nearly blew it. I ain't used ta bein' around nice girls. I hope she din't hear what I almost said. I gotta watch what I say and do. I was so deep in thought I almost didn't hear Cheryl's response.

"Sure you can. It's a slow dance. You just stand close and rock back and forth. Come on, I'll show you." She took my hand and we headed for the dance floor. I tried not to step on her feet. She was nice, tellin' me how to hold her and jus' kinda rock back and forth until I got the hang of it. I din't know what to say, but she kept talkin' like she din't notice that I wasn't sayin' much'. Finally she said,

"I'm going to band camp this summer. I play the flute. I go to the camp every summer so I know all the kids. I sure can't wait to see them again. What are you going to do this summer?"

"I'm goin' to O'Shea for the summer with my grandparents and my Mama. We're goin' to Virginia Beach for a week, too. Have you ever been there?" I was shocked that she had gotten three sentences out of me. I think she was, too. I just din't know how to talk to a girl, but I have to admit, it felt nice holdin' one, even if it was only for one dance. Too soon the music ended, and we rejoined Barry and Rebecca. I din't know what to do next. I wanted to dance with her again, but I wasn't sure if she wanted to dance with me. Were there rules for this that I din't know? I din't want to ask her and get turned down. So we just stood and talked. But I noticed she din't walk away from me. So when the next song came on, and Rebecca and Barry went to dance, I took a chance.

"Um.. do you want to dance again?" My palms were sweaty, and I wiped them on my pants. I hoped she din't notice.

"Sure." This was a fast dance. I sorta knew how to do this one, and we din't have to hold hands, so she wouldn't see how nervous I was. After that we danced together for the rest of the night. I was still strugglin' with conversation, but she din't seem to care. Then it came to the countdown for midnight. I wasn't sure what to do. Did she want me to kiss her? I sure din't want to get slapped! 5…4…3…2…1… Happy New Year! She leaned in and gave me a little kiss on the cheek. So I gave her one, too. It felt nice, really nice. When the last dance was over, I asked her if she wanted me to walk her home.

"Sure, that would be nice. But I have to call my parents and tell them not to come and get me. " We found a phone, I gave her a dime, and she called home. Then I realized that I'd forgotten all about Mama. But she musta been watchin' me. She came over.

"Tommy, Mr. and Mrs. Brenner will take me home. You take your time with your friend. I'll be waiting for you when you get home."

"Thank, Ma. Oh, this is Cheryl Ames."

"Nice to meet you Cheryl."

"Nice to meet you, too, Mrs. Thompson." I could see Mama wince at that name. She hated it, but she was stuck with it."

Cheryl got her coat. I saw Barry help Rebecca on with her cape, so I helped Cheryl on with her coat. I wish I knew the rules for how to treat a girl right. I surely never learned from watchin' Snake. We walked out into the cold midnight air.

"I live down on Oak Street," Cheryl said. "It's in the opposite direction from your house."

"That's okay. Anyway we aren't stayin' at the old house. We rented a place on Elm for the rest of the year, so I'm only a block away from you." Her hand brushed against mine. I wasn't sure if it was an accident, but I took the chance. I held her hand. She din't pull away. What I had thought would never happen, was happening. I was a normal guy, walkin' a girl home from a dance. It was amazin' how happy somethin' that simple made me feel. When we approached her door, I started to panic again. What was I supposed to do now? I knew what I wanted to do. I wanted to kiss her, a real kiss. But she was a nice girl. I din't think I should do that. This wasn't even a real date. So I did something really corny that I saw in the movies. I kissed her hand. Then I was like to die of embarrassment. That was so lame. How could I have done that? But Cheryl smiled. She seemed pleased and surprised.

"Um… I'd like to see you again…. If you want to." I stuttered.

"Sure, I'd like that."

I ran the block to my house. She wanted to see me again. I had a girl-friend. Who'da ever thought. But I hafta talk to Barry and find out what I was supposed to do. Find out what the rules are with girls. Mama was waitin' for me when I got home. That was a nice feelin', too. Someone carin' when I came home, or even if I came home.

"So you had a good time. I told you if you were nice to people they'd be nice back. Cheryl seems nice."

"Yeah, she is! Mama, I want to go out with her again. But I don't know how to treat a girl. What do I do? What do I say? I don't want to do anything wrong."

"Tommyboy, just be yourself. I mean there are little things like opening doors for her and helping her on with her coat, and paying for things when you go out together. Listening to her when she talks. Girls like that. And you always treat her with respect. Believe she means "no" when she say "no," and never try to force her to do anything she doesn't want to do." Her voice drifted off there, and I wasn't sure if she was talking about how I should treat Cheryl or how Snake shoulda treated her.

"Mama, I would never do anything with Cheryl. That's what girls like Anytime April are for."

"No! And don't let me hear you call her that again. You don't treat any girl with disrespect, even those who don't seem to respect themselves. You don't know what made her the way she is. People judged you by your actions when they didn't know what was going on in your life to make you the way you were. Don't do the same to April or anyone else. Usually when someone acts like that girl does, there is a reason for it."

"Yes, Mama." I could see I couldn't have the conversation I wanted to have. I couldn't ask Mama when it would be all right to kiss Cheryl or put my arm around her waist. I decided I'd ask Barry.

"Good Night, Mama."

"Good night, Tommyboy."

Saturday Date I

"Saturday's child has to work for its living."
From Monday's Child is Fair of Face - Anonymous

Tommy approached me in school.

"I want to take Cheryl out, but how can I tell if she even wants to go out with me? I mean after the dance she said she wanted to see me again, but maybe she was just bein' polite."

"I can find out from Becky. They tell each other everything."

"But can she find out without tellin' Cheryl that I want to take her out. I don't want her to know I like her until I know she likes me, too." It was almost funny and a little sad to see Tommy so insecure.

"I'm pretty sure Cheryl likes you, but I'll find out from Becky. I promise I won't mention that you want to take Cheryl out." The funny thing is, when I saw Becky, she asked me if Tommy had said anything about Cheryl. It turns out Cheryl had asked her to find out from me if Tommy liked her!

When I reported the conversation to Tommy, he grinned ear to ear. That was a sight I'd have to get used to. The scowl that used to be permanently set on his face was gone.

"I was hopin' you'd double date with us. I don't know the rules for dating. I can watch you and Rebecca, and I'll know what to do. I never know what to say." I thought it was pretty funny that Tommy considered me an expert on girls, and I told him so.

"Don't worry about what to say. The girls will do most of the talking! Just listen to them, and nod once in a while." But I agreed to the double date. Tommy and Cheryl and Becky and I made a date to bowl the next Saturday. I had my $5.00 allowance for the week, and I helped my Pa in his store that morning to make a little extra money.

On Saturday, we stopped at the record store on the way to the bowling alley. I knew Becky wanted a copy of our song, and she also wanted "Bobby's Girl." I also wanted a copy of "Can't Help Falling in Love With You. I don't buy many records, like Becky does, but that was our song, so I had to have that one. The 45 records were on sale, three for $1.50. I splurged and bought them for us. Tommy got Cheryl the record she wanted, "He's A Rebel."

Then we headed to the bowling alley. Games were three for a dollar, so we decided to play three. I had to figure what I could afford and still have money to go for sodas afterwards. I liked having a girlfriend, but it sure was expensive. By the time I took Becky home, my allowance was gone. It was a good thing I'd picked up the extra $5.00 working.

SATURDAY DATE: II

"We cared for each other as Child and Maid"
by Heinrich Heine

Should I call Cheryl? Should I stop by her house? What should I say when I see her in school? Did she really want me to call her again or was she just being polite. What if she told someone I kissed her hand? Maybe all the kids in school were laughin' at me. I looked for Barry as soon as I got to the schoolyard.

"I need your help. Did Cheryl say anything to Rebecca about me? I want to take Cheryl out, but how can I tell if she even wants to go out with me? I mean after the dance she said she wanted to see me again, but maybe she was just bein' polite."

"Slow down. That's the most I've heard you say at one time since I met you! I think Cheryl liked you, but I'll ask Becky. They tell each other everything."

"But can she find out without tellin' Cheryl that I want to take her out. I don't want her to know I like her until I know she likes me, too." I wondered if datin' was worth it. I din't like feelin' so jittery. But anyway Barry came back and told me that Cheryl asked Rebecca if I had said anything about her, so I guess she does like me. I wonder if I looked as relieved as I felt. But then I had a new problem. I wanted to ask her out, but what should I say? Where should we go?

"Barry, I need another favor. I was hopin' you'd double date with us. I don't know the rules for datin'. I can watch you and Rebecca, and I'll know what to do. I never know what to say." Barry laughed.

"I can't believe you are asking me for advice on dating. Becky is the first girl I've ever dated. I don't know any more than you do! But I'll be glad to double-date with you and Cheryl. Becky and I were talking about going bowling on Saturday. Do you want to do that?"

"I guess. Do you think Cheryl will like that?"

"Yeah. She and Becky used to bowl every weekend."

"Oh! I'm not that good at it. I never had the money to go. I don't want to look like an idiot."

"Don't worry about it. I'm not that good either, and we're just going to have some fun."

"How do I ask her?"

"Come with me. She's with Becky. I'll remind Becky we are going on Saturday and then you can ask Cheryl if she wants to go, too." We walked over to the girls. Barry asked,

"Becks, are we still going bowling on Saturday?"

"Yes."

I said, "That sounds like fun. Cheryl, do you want to go, too?"

"Sure." She flashed me a Cheshire cat smile. And I know I was just a grinnin' fool.

Grandpa was in town for the weekend and he gave me $20 for the date. I'd never had a spare dollar to spend, and here I was with $20. I felt like a millionaire.

When I went to pick Cheryl up, her father asked me to come in. I could tell he was checkin' me out. Her father took me aside.

"Young man, I'm giving you the benefit of the doubt. I have to tell you I was less than thrilled when Cheryl told me she wanted to go out with you. I've seen you around for years, and you aren't what I had in mind for my daughter. But recently, you've cleaned up nicely. And Cheryl says you were a perfect gentleman when you brought her home on New Year's. I expect you will continue to be."

"Oh, yes, Sir."

"And you are going with Barry and Rebecca, right?"

"Yes, Sir. They should be here any minute."

"Okay then." He called upstairs, "Cheryl, your young man is here." Cheryl rolled her eyes at her dad as she came down the steps. I fought off the nervous laughter that was just below the surface. Just then the bell rang. It was Barry and Rebecca. I breathed an audible sigh of relief as we stepped out of the house. Barry and Rebecca walked a little ahead of us. We hung back a little.

"I'm sorry about that," Cheryl whispered. "Dad's a little over-protective. I'm sure he gave you the third degree."

"I can't say I blame him. With the reputation I have, if I had a daughter, I woun't let her go out with me."

"But you've changed. I used to be afraid of you. You always seemed so angry. But on New Year's you were really sweet."

"Well don't go public with that. I have a reputation to protect."

"Sure! Your secret is safe with me. I don't want any other girls to find out how nice you can be." We picked up our pace to walk with Barry and Rebecca. When we stopped at the record shop, Barry bought Becky a couple of records. I could see him counting his money to make sure he'd have enough for later. I never thought I'd be feelin' sorry for Barry! I bought Cheryl a record, too. She wanted "He's A Rebel" because it reminded her of how I used to be. I saw Barry raise his eyebrows when I pulled out that $20. I felt important, but I brushed it off. I din't want Barry to feel bad.

"My Grandpa's makin' up for lost time. I guess he's spoilin' me a little to make up for all the years I din't have noth…anything."

At the bowling alley, we laughed and laughed. I wasn't bad for someone who'd only bowled once or twice in his whole life. But it was fun. The girls were good. They were the experts, so we let them keep score. They were talking about joining the bowling team in High School. When it came time to pay, I saw Barry counting out the money again. I whispered to him,

"I can lend you some if you're short."

"Boy, things sure have changed for you, haven't they?" he replied.

"They sure have. I went from poor as dirt to rich as Midas. Trust me, rich is better. So do you need a loan?"

"Thanks, but I'm okay. I worked in my dad's store this morning, so I have a little extra money. I just have to make sure to keep a little for the rest of the week."

"What do we do now?"

"We ask the girls if they want to stop at Woolworth's for a soda." Just then the girls returned from powdering their noses. I wondered why they called it that. They weren't wearing any make-up that I could see. I walked over to Cheryl.

"Do you want to go for a soda?"

"Sure." I saw Barry reach for Becky's hand, so I reached for Cheryl's. We walked hand-in- hand down Main Street. The manager of Woolworth's, who always used to keep his eye on me whenever I entered the store, didn't even give me a second glance. I don't think he recognized me. We sat at the soda fountain and drank an ice cream soda with two straws. I told her she could order her own if she wanted, but she said,

"It's more fun to share." She was right. And when we both put our straws in the same glass, Cheryl was announcin' to everyone that she was there with me. I liked that. Then we walked home. I got nervous again when we parted ways. Barry was takin' Becky home, and Cheryl and I lived in a different direction. As we approached Cheryl's door, my panic mounted. What was I supposed to do now? Did I try to kiss her? Why didn't anyone ever write a rule book about this stuff? I took a deep breath as we got to her doorway. We'd already kissed on the cheek on New Year's. I'd already kissed her hand. I decided to try for the real thing. I leaned in; so did she. Our noses bumped!

"Oh no, I'm sorry."

"It's okay." We shared a nervous laugh, and it occurred to me that maybe she was just as unsure as I was. We tried again, and this time we got it right. A short kiss, but nice.

"Um, do you want to go out with me again?"

"Sure! I had a really good time today."

"Me, too."

The Trial: I

There's Grief of Want-and Grief of Cold-
A sort they call "Despair"-
There's Banishment from native Eyes-
In sight of Native Air-

Emily Dickinson

The story of Mrs. Thompson being kept prisoner for seven years was national news, and Snake's trial was billed as "The Trial of the Century." There were cameras and newspaper reporters swarming all over the courthouse when we arrived. My Ma and Pa walked in with me, and shielded me. But poor Tommy and his Ma were swallowed up by the reporters all shouting questions at them. My legs were like Jello when the lawyer called me to the stand. I felt the weight of the words pressing down on me when I put my hand on the Bible and said,

"I swear to tell the truth, the whole truth, and nothing but the truth, so help me God." All those people watching and the jury and the judge and the newspaper men. My voice squeaked and broke as I described the day I picked Tommy up to go to the library and saw Snake whaling on him. Then they asked me about the day, we dug the stuff up in the garden, and the sheriff came and took Mrs. Thompson out of the shed. I'd tried to forget that shed. I'd tried to forget what she looked like. A skeleton in rags. But the memories all came back when I testified. The sheriff carrying her out of the shed like a big rag doll.

The defense attorney wasn't too bad. I think he knew scaring a kid wouldn't help him with the jury. Still I was glad when it was over. Then Tommy had to go on the stand. He had guts. He looked Snake square in the eyes. He told about life with Snake and his mom. He told about beatings and exile to the cave after his mom disappeared. He talked about Snake's drinking and making moonshine and robbing houses.

The sheriff got on the stand, talking about finding Mrs. Thompson in the shed. His voice broke as he described the way she looked when he found her. He apologized again for not searching for her sooner, even though a missing person report had not been filed. Ma testified, too. She talked about the last day she saw Mrs. Thompson before she disappeared. And the way Mrs. Thompson looked when she was first rescued.

Finally Mrs. Thompson, still painfully thin, sat in the witness chair. Her hair, still in the process of growing in, was in little red ringlets. At first, she tried to avert her eyes from her husband, her tormentor. She focused on the lawyer's questions.

Lawyer: How did you meet John Thompson?

Mary: My father was the Mayor of O'Shea, Virginia where I lived. He also owned a furniture store in town. Snake...um...John was a handyman who did odd jobs in the City Hall Building, and also in my father's store. One day I was playing the piano in the store and John heard me. We started talking.

Lawyer: How old were you?

Mary: Seventeen. I was a senior at O'Shea High School.

Lawyer: You were actually a piano prodigy, were you not?

Mary: I played some concerts. I'd been accepted at Julliard for the following fall.

Lawyer: But you never attended Julliard, did you?

Mary: No. John and I got married.

Lawyer: You, a wealthy socialite, granddaughter of the founding father of the town, daughter of the mayor, child prodigy married the janitor? How did that happen?

Mary: One day my father mentioned that John was out sick. I thought it would be nice if I took him some soup. I went to his room and he misunderstood my intentions. I was just trying to be nice. He thought a young girl who comes to a man's room is there for something else. I said, "No." He thought I was just being coy. I got pregnant.

Lawyer: He raped you?

Mary: I hate that word, but, yes, he forced me.

Lawyer: Did you report it to the police?

Mary. No.

Lawyer: Did you tell your parents?

Mary: No.

Lawyer: Why not?

Mary: I was ashamed. Snake said it was my word against his. He said nice girls didn't go to a man's room alone. If I told, and no one believed me, I'd be an outcast. Even if they believed me, no decent boy would ever go out with me after that. It was different in 1948. Nice girls didn't get pregnant. And my father was Mayor. His political enemies would have had a field day. My father would have been so disappointed in me. I just couldn't tell anyone. When Snake said he'd marry me, I didn't see any other way. I think he expected my father to support us and give him a better job. So we eloped.

Lawyer: Why do you call John, Snake?

Mary: (Her face turned the color of her hair. She turned to the judge.) Do I have to answer that? It's embarrassing.

Judge (kindly) Yes, you do.

Mary: The day he…, the day he got me pregnant, before he would let me leave his apartment, he told me he called his… um… thing, Snake. He told me from then on I was to call him Snake, so I'd always remember what happened that day… As if I could ever forget."

I felt so bad for her. Her face was the color of her hair, and her voice was barely a whisper. I didn't know how Tommy could stand it.

Lawyer: So what happened after you eloped?

Mary: My parents threw me out when I told them I eloped. I never told them I was pregnant. Pride, I guess. I didn't want them to know I had to get married, and I just couldn't tell them how it happened. All I got was my violin, my piano, and my clothes. Snake was furious. I was married to a violent man who scared me. But he made it clear I was his, and I'd better never think of leaving him.

Lawyer: What was your marriage like?

Mary: Snake was demanding, obsessive, abusive. He drank. I couldn't go out without his permission. Dinner had to be on the table when he came home. When he called the house, I'd better be there to answer it. My marriage was a prison. When he wanted me, I was to be there. Not even our son could come before Snake's needs. After the day he…forced me, he refused to call me Mary. He said Mary had been a virgin, and I wasn't. He started called me Maggie. He said it was short for Mary Magdalene, the fallen woman. I hated that name, but when we moved here, he told people that was my name. And I had learned better than to challenge him about anything.

Lawyer: Didn't you ever try to leave?

Mary: I didn't have any money. I didn't have anywhere to go. My parents didn't know about Tommy. I wasn't sure they'd take us in. And Snake had also said he'd kill me if I tried to leave him. But then when Tommy was six, Snake was sent to prison. Those were the best six months of my life, and Tommy's, too. I gave piano lessons and made some money. Tommy just blossomed. And I knew I had to get away for Tommy's sake. But Snake got out of prison early. He came in when I was packing. He beat the daylights out of me. Called me a whore. Told me I'd never leave him. I think he would have killed me, but I shouted at him. "Go ahead. Kill me. At least I'll be free from you." Then he stopped cold. He said, "No, you'll never be free from me." He dragged me by the hair to the shed in the yard and locked me in. He told me if I ever let anyone know I was there or if I tried to escape, he'd kill Tommy. He said, "You're mine 'til you die."   That was in 1955.

Lawyer: And you were in that shed all that time? How did you survive?

Mary: For the first six years, when Tommy was in school, Snake would bring me in the house. I could shower, wash my hair, but then I had to take care of him, and take care of the house. I really was a slave. I scrubbed the floors, cooked the meals, did the laundry. I would cook these wonderful gourmet meals for him. I had to hand feed him, but I wasn't allowed to have any. He would throw his leftovers in the garbage. One time he caught me sneaking some out of the trash. He beat me and starved me for two days. He kept me working until it was almost time for Tommy to come home, then he'd lock me back in the shed with cold canned food and bottles of water.

Lawyer: You said this went on for six years. What happened the seventh?

Mary: He forgot me for a few days. I was filthy, hungry. When he came back, I had head lice. That disgusted him. He's always loved my mop of red hair, but that day, he brought scissors and made me crop my hair. From then on, he wasn't interested in me anymore. He didn't want me to bring my filthy infested body into the house. That last year I almost never left the shed. He came less and less often to bring me food. I had a bucket for a toilet. The shed smelled. I smelled. I wanted to wash my clothes. I wanted to wash myself, but I never knew when he was going to come back with more water. I had to save the water to drink. I lived like an animal for that last year. He'd forget to feed me for days, but he didn't want me to die. He wanted me to suffer. He seemed to know how to keep me just on the brink of death without letting me die. And then finally Tommy had Snake arrested for beating him. My son convinced the sheriff that I hadn't left him. And the sheriff, with Tommy and Barry's help, found me.

Everyone in the court room was in tears. I watched Tommy's face through the whole proceedings. It was all there; the agony of hearing again that he was the child of rape. The horror of what his father had done to his mother. And the love for his mother was written on his face as well. He finally understood that she had never abandoned him. The guilt he felt that that she had sacrificed her own freedom to keep him safe. He had kept his emotions suppresses for seven years. In all that time, whenever they burst through, it was in the form of rage. Now the emotions were all there, raw, in his face. I hurt for him, but I knew better than to show it. Tommy would never tolerate pity.

When the trial was over, Snake was sentenced to 15 years in prison with no possibility of parole for at least 7 ½ years. But what really got Snake's goat was when the judge informed him that under Virginia law, Mrs. Thompson could apply for an uncontested divorce and petition to take back her maiden name, Mary O'Shea. Tommy asked the judge if he could change his name to O'Shea also. He was allowed to change it to Tommy O'Shea Thompson. But the judge said when he is 21, he will have the right to drop the Thompson altogether if he still wants to.

The Trial: II

There is but one law for all, namely, that law which governs all law, the law of our creator, the law of humanity, justice, equity.

Edmund Burke from Impeachment of Warren Hastings.

The trial was the worst few days of my life, and the best. I felt a sense of power when I got on the stand to testify against Snake. I was still terrified of him. I knew if somehow he was set free, he'd kill Ma and me. But I had to do this for Ma, and for myself. We'd both been his victims for the past seven years. I looked Snake right in the eyes, and I was looking at pure evil. My heart was pounding but I refuse to let my voice quiver. I told the court about the beatings, the moonshine, the hole, and the things he said and did the day Ma disappeared. I told about the house. How it had been spotlessly clean for the first six years, and filthy for the last. Of course, now I understood why. How Snake had assigned me the household chores during the last year, and punished me when the house wasn't cleaned perfectly.

I listened to Barry on the stand. I heard his mother recount the last day she had seen my mother before her disappearance. I saw the sheriff close to tears again as he recalled the day he freed my mother from the shed.

But I nearly lost it when Ma testified. Her hair was still growing in. It was in red Shirley Temple ringlets. She was still so thin that she looked like a child on the stand. At first, her voice was barely a whisper. She seemed afraid to look at Snake, but as she spoke, her voice got stronger and her eyes flashed. I was watching her reclaim her dignity, her freedom, herself. I was proud of her. I was furious at Snake. My emotions were a jumble. It hurt to hear her testimony. My fists clenched, my head throbbed, as I heard the awful things that Snake had done to her. I fought back my tears when I heard her tell how she tolerated the abuse for all those years to protect me. I felt love, rage, shame, pride all at the same time. I'd always believed no one could hurt me worse than Snake, but I was wrong. Hearing about Mama's love for me, and her suffering because of it, wounded me more than anything Snake had ever done to me.

Snake insisted on speaking. His defense lawyer asked him to tell about his early life.

"I never know'd my folks. Never had a family of my own. I was raised in orphanages and foster homes. Ran off when I was sixteen and been supportin' myself ever since. Then I got to O'Shea. Mayor gave me a job in his store and I seen Mary there. She was the prettiest thing I ever seen, with that mop of red hair. And she played the piano like an angel. I knowed the first time I saw her, I wanted her. She didn't act better 'n me. Talked to me nice, so I figured she liked me, too. Then the day she come to my room when I was sick, I knowed for sure. Girls don't come to yer room lessen they like ya. 'Specially nice girls like Mary. So I pulled her to me, to show I wanted her, too. And she said, No!" Figured she was just bein' cute, not wantin' to seem to want it too much. Then afterwards, she cried and shrank away from me like I had the plague. Said she was gonna call the police. I knowed then she was a tease like every other woman, thinkin' she was too good for the likes of me. But she was mine, and she was always gonna be mine. She was my chance to finally have a family of my own. I had to bring her down a peg. Remind her she was spoilt now and no other man would want her. So I called her Maggie and made her call me Snake. It musta worked. As far as I know she never told nobody what happened that day. Then miracle of miracles, she comes back and tells me she's pregnant. I'll admit I was pretty mean. Made her beg me to marry her. But that was just payback for makin' me feel like dirt. I was glad to marry her. Glad to have a baby comin'. Now I'd have a family of my own. Have people who had to love me.

But she didn't. She cringed every time I touched her. My wife. She shoulda loved me. I made an honest woman of her and the kid. But she'd stiffen up every time I touched her. So I made her love me. It was my right. She was my wife. She belonged to me. She loved the kid though. Boy did she love that kid. But she never loved me, and neither did he. So maybe I wasn't the best husband or father, I never had nobody show me how. But they was mine, and I was gonna keep 'em. Then one day I come home from jail, and she's packin' up to leave. And gonna take the kid, too. I couldn't let 'er leave. She wasn't gonna take my family from me and leave me alone again. I never did nothin' wrong. She is my wife and Tommy is my kid. I have the right to punish them when they misbehave. Any man would do the same to keep what is his. And I know my rights. My wife and son shou'nta been allowed to testify against me. My lawyer says there should be a mistrial."

I could hardly breathe when he spoke. If the court agreed with him, much of the case would disappear, and I feared he could actually go free. The judge called for a two hour adjournment while he studied the request.

My heart was in my throat for those two hours. Could Snake really get off? If he did, Mama and I would never be safe. But when the judge returned, he cited a 1950 decision that said while a wife cannot be forced to testify against her husband, she can do so voluntarily. Snake went wild! He shrieked at the judge,

"I din't do anything wrong. I was just keepin' what was mine. You just wait, I'll make them pay, and you'd better watch your back, too, 'cause I'll get out someday and I'll be comin' after ya." The Judge banged the gavel.

"Sit down and shut up or I will hold you in contempt." But Snake just kept on rantin' even while two policemen were draggin' him out of court in handcuffs. When Snake spoke again of his right as master of the house to discipline his wife and son as he saw fit, it occurred to me that he truly didn't believe that he had done anything wrong. The depth of his evil frightened me. I'd heard the word sociopath. Now I knew what it meant. I was lookin' at one. What was worse, those genes were in me. I knew I had been guilty of cruelty. I'd been guilty of theft. I'd been a bully. I was terrified that I could become Snake. My mom said I had her genes, too. That I had a choice about the kind of person I wanted to be. But did I? The thought tormented me. I'd rather be dead than be like Snake. And that, I realized, was the proof that my mother was right. Snake had no guilt, no remorse. I did.

When the trial was over, I looked for those I'd hurt. I found the little Jones boy and told him I was sorry. I bought him some candy to make up for the Halloween candy I'd taken from him the year before. I went to Mr. Brenner and paid him for all the goods I could remember stealing from his store. I even apologized to the kids I'd beat up at school last year, even though they had insulted me first. Of course, I apologized to Barry, but he just brushed it off.

"We both grew up a lot this year," he said. "I misjudged you; you mistreated me, but we got past it. I'm glad I got to know you this year."

"Me, too." I felt better. If I was sorry, then I wasn't like Snake. I still had to set things right with God, though. I hadn't been to confession in seven years.

Ma and I both spoke during the sentencing phase of the trial. We both told the court how much we had lost together because of Snake's actions. We told the court that we would never be safe if Snake ever got free. Snake's own ranting and threats to the judge helped convince the judge that Snake posed a very real danger to our lives, and his. Ma and I were relieved beyond words when Snake was sentenced to 15 years in prison. In addition, if he is ever paroled, Grandpa promised to get the town of O'Shea to issue a restraining order forbidding Snake to ever contact or come near either of us. Just the word *parole* sent chills down my spine. I knew no piece of paper would keep him from coming after us if he ever got out. But he wouldn't even be eligible for parole for 7 ½ years, so I won't worry about that now. I'll just try to be glad he is finally out of our lives. Seems right somehow that he can't even try for parole for seven years seeing that he took seven years of my mother's life.

Ma, in her closing statement before sentencing for Snake, had told the judge that she wanted a divorce, and she knew Snake would never give her one. But the judge told her and Snake that under some Virginia law, because Snake was guilty of "cruelty and inflicting bodily harm," Ma could apply for an uncontested divorce. I think that was a worse punishment than the jail time. Snake did not like to give up what he considered his. And he thought he owned Ma and me. For Ma, that order really set her free. After the trial, she petitioned the court for the right to return to her maiden name Mary O'Shea. I asked the court if I could use the name O'Shea, too. After the awful details released at Snake's trial, the judge sympathized with me, but he said I could not give up the last name Thompson without my father's permission. I knew Snake would never agree. As far as he was concerned, I, like my mother, belonged to him. Not that he loved me or anything, but I was his possession and he wouldn't relinquish me willingly. The judge did allow me to take the name Thomas O'Shea Thompson, and he told me that once I turn 21, I wouldn't need Snake's permission to change my name. I can wait. I will be totally free from Snake in seven years, and hopefully, he will still be in jail.

School Days: I

"Beginning my studies, the first step pleased me so much."
"Beginning my Studies" in **Leaves of Grass** *by Walt Whitman*

When they trial was over, life went on. The day came for Tommy and me to present our report to the class. My parents and Tommy's ma and grandparents were there when Tommy and I did our state presentation. My hands were shaking. My voice was cracking. I was sick to my stomach at the thought of speaking in front of people. But Tommy was all smiles. I think he was actually looking forward to it. I made the posters for our talk. We hung them around the room. And Tommy took the facts we had researched, and set them in rhyme. We took a deep breath and began.

> There are facts about Texas we want you to know.
> You'll learn about Houston, Austin, San Antonio.
> So welcome to Texas, the Lone Star State
> It has 1/12th the land mass of the Continental 48.
> It was once the largest state from Florida to Nebraska
> Till 1959, when statehood came to Alaska.
> It's famous for cotton and oil and cattle,
> For chemical plants, and the Alamo battle.

Once we got into the rhythm, the presentation just sailed along, and I forgot to be nervous. When we were done, the class gave us a standing ovation. Miss Jenkins said it was the most innovative and informative report she had ever heard. After two other reports were given, Miss Jenkins announced a treat for the class. Tommy's mother was going to play the piano and sing for us. When she sang, I recognized the words from Tommy's notebook. His mother had set his lyrics to music. Our usually restless class listened in absolute silence. When she finished, the class burst into applause. Ted said, "Wow!" when Mrs. Thompson, uh, I mean O'Shea, told the class that Tommy had written the words. We were all really impressed when Miss Jenkins asked them, "Will you perform your song at the graduation assembly?"

His mother looked at Tommy. He nodded. "We'd love to perform at the graduation," she replied.

School Days: II

Only a lot of boys and girls?
Only the tiresome spelling, writing, ciphering classes?
Only a public school?
Ah, more, infinitely more;
*   "An Old Man's Thought of School" in* **Leaves of Grass** *by*
*   Walt Whitman*

It was tough gettin' back into school work after the trial. The whole experience had been such a rollercoaster for me. But Barry and I worked hard on our project. For the presentation I figured we should try something new. Most of the talks were so borin' I was ready to nod off. I wanted ours to be different. So I told Barry I wanted to set the whole talk to rhyme. As soon as the words were out of my mouth, I wanted him to talk me out of it. I didn't know how the class or the teacher would receive it, and I was scared. If we failed it would be my fault. Besides, except when I teased Barry, no one had heard my rhymes before. Suppose they laughed at me?

"Never mind," I said. That was stupid idea."

"No, it was a brilliant idea. Do you think you can do it?"

"I guess."

"Great! And I'll make posters for the main points we want to make. We can hang them around the room. When we get to a particular point in the presentation, we can stand next to the poster that illustrates what we are talking about."

"This could be really cool!"

When the day came, my stomach was hurtin.' My palms were sweaty. But I pasted a smile on my face so no one would know. Barry's hands were shakin' and so was his voice. To make it worse, family had been invited to the talks. My Mama and grandparents were there. But once we started the rhyme, we got caught in the rhythm of it, and out voices got stronger. When we were done, the whole class stood up and clapped. Imagine that! The class was applauding for me. When the other presentations were finished, Miss Jenkins announced a surprise. My Mama played the piano for the class. It was a surprise for me, too. She set one of my poems to music and sang as she played. I was so proud, I'm surprised my shirt buttons din't pop when Mama announced to the class that she wrote the music and I wrote the words. And then Miss Jenkins asked Mama and me if we would perform our song together at graduation. Afterwards all the kids were comin' up to me like they were my best friends.

"That was cool! I didn't know you wrote songs," Ted said.

"You sure can write! Do you think you could write me a song?" asked Cheryl.

"I can try." It felt strange to suddenly be popular.

"Now that you are a famous composer, do you think you'll still have time for your lowly old friends?" Barry asked. I knew he was teasin'. Tryin' to keep me from gettin' a swelled head.

"Yeah, and maybe if you play your cards right, I'll let you design my first album cover." It was still strange to engage in friendly teasing. It was a new experience for me, but I liked it.

Later that day, Cheryl came burstin' out of the girls' room.

"You won't believe what I just heard. It's a good thing you decided to leave April alone."

"Why, what did you hear?"

"Well, I was in the girls' room and two of the cheerleaders came in, you know Sharon and Joan. I guess they thought they were alone in there. And Sharon tells Joan,

'Did you hear about April?'

And Joan says, 'Hear what about April?'

And Sharon says, 'You remember that soldier Jerry that April was so crazy about?'

'Yeah,' says Joan, 'I never could figure out what a nineteen year old was doing hanging around a fourteen year old.'

'Well I can tell you what he was doing! Seems when he was stationed in Korea, he was no more faithful to April than she was to him. Anyway he comes home on leave in March, they get together, and before he returns to Korea, he leaves her a little going away present, if you get my drift.'

And Joan says, 'Oh, my God! You mean she's preggers?'

And Sharon says, 'No it's worse than that. He left her with a dose!'

And good old slow-witted Joan asks, 'A dose of what?'

Sharon says all sarcastic-like, 'A dose! The clap!'

And Joan still doesn't get it, so Sharon finally shouts 'VD! You know venereal disease. Gosh, you're dense sometimes!' Anyway I waited till they left the room, and I came out to tell you. Can you believe it?"

"Yeah! I can believe it. What I can't believe is that I actually feel sorry for April. When this gets around, no one will go near her. I hope you won't be the one to spread the news."

"I thought you'd be glad after the way she treated you to see her get her due. And as for spreading the news, the high school boys have a right to know, so they'll stay away from her."

"You have a point, and knowing Sharon and Joan, I am sure everyone in town will know by tomorrow. But we don't have to be the ones to spread the gossip."

DOUBTS I

"My life is in the hands of any fool who makes me lose my temper."

Joseph Hunter

Things were goin' too good for me. Ma was home. Cheryl and me were goin' good. I was even doin' good in school. Shoulda known it woun't last. Today started out okay. When school was over, Cheryl stayed for band practice. Barry's Ma wasn't feelin' good, so he went home to help her. So I walked home alone. I guess when I seen Beau Stuart, I shoulda walked the other way. But I did send him a note a ways back sayin' I was sorry for givin' him a whuppin' last year. Anyways I walked by and he starts jawin' at me.

"Well, Tommy Thompson, aren't you just the dandy in those fancy clothes of yours."

"Beau, why you want to start messin' with me? I tole you I was sorry 'bout last year."

"You may fool the others with your money and fancy clothes, but not me. On the inside, you're still the same rag boy you always were. Your Pa's no good white trash, and you're just like him."

Then it happened. I could feel my face turnin' red. Felt the jaw clench. Felt that vein throbbin' on the side of my temple. Felt my hands roll into fists. Then as if it had a mind of its own, the right fist shot out.

Just as fast, the fists uncurled, and I took off runnin'. My fist was throbbin'. My head was poundin'. Those words kept echoin' in my brain. "You're Pa's no good white trash, and you're just like him." And I knew he was right. I just proved he was right. Din't know where I was runnin' 'til I got there. Moved the rock, slid the board aside, and climbed back into my hole where I belonged.

Doubts II

"Who is strong? He who subdues his evil impulses."
Pirke Avot *4:1*

Ma was feeling poorly again, so I went home to help her with dinner. It must have been about 6:30 when the phone rang. It was Tommy's Ma. Tommy hadn't come home for dinner. She asked if he was with me. I could tell she was upset when I said I hadn't seen him. She said,

"I'm worried. He hasn't done anything like this before. And I just got a call from Mrs. Stuart. She said she's going to call the Sheriff. It seems Tommy took a swing at Beau today."

"Oh, geez! Is Beau hurt bad?"

"No, that's the strange thing. Tommy didn't actually hit Beau. He punched the fence right by Beau's face."

I exhaled loudly. I don't know why I felt so relieved.

"So why is she calling the Sheriff? Is the fence going to press charges?"

"This is no joke, Barry."

"I know, Ma'am. I'm sorry. But I can't help thinking Beau did or said something, because Tommy hasn't lost his temper like that since you've been back."

"I can't have Tommy acting like that, no matter what the Stuart boy did or said."

"I know, Ma'am."

"I'm really getting worried. Do you know where Tommy might have gone?"

And suddenly it hit me. I knew exactly where Tommy was.

"I think so. It might be better if I go get him. He's probably ashamed of what he did."

"Please call me as soon as you know anything."

"I will."

"What was that about?" Ma asked.

"That was Tommy's ma. Tommy's in trouble. As soon as Pa gets here, I have to go look for him. I think I know where he is."

"Well what are you waiting for? Get going. I'm feeling better now and Pa will be home any minute."

I got on my bike and pedaled like demons were chasing me. When I got to the woods, the stone had been removed and the board pushed aside. I knew I had found him.

"Tommy! Tommy! You in there?"

When I didn't get an answer, some scary memories came flashing back.

"Tommy!" I shouted louder.

"Go away! I wanna be alone."

"I'm coming in. I heard that once you've saved somebody's life, you're responsible for him for life. So you're stuck with me."

"Whaddaya want?"

"I don't want anything, but your mother wants you to come home. She called my house looking for you, and she was really worried."

"I can't go home. Ma will be so disappointed in me. I can't control my temper. I'm afraid I'll just wind up hurting her like Snake did."

"I'm no expert on parents, but I think you're hurting her right now."

"You don't understand."

"So explain it to me. Does this have anything to do with what happened today with Beau Stuart? I hear you scared the crap out of him today. Literally!"

"How do you know about that?"

"Mrs. Stuart called your Ma. She called me. So tell me what happened."

"Beau saw me in the street and started on me for wearing nice clothes. Then he said that I could fool other people, but I couldn't fool him. That underneath the fancy clothes, I was still the same Rag Boy I'd always been, and that I was nothing but no good white trash just like my father. That's when I swung at him."

"Why? Because he said the words, or because deep down you believed them?"

"What are you, a psychologist? Besides he was right, wasn't he? I proved that today."

"No, actually you proved he was wrong today."

"How do you figure that?"

"He gave you every reason to beat him to a pulp, which is exactly what Snake would have done in that situation. But you didn't. You punched the fence instead. Not that that was the smartest way to deal with the situation.

In fact, judging by the condition of your knuckles, it was a pretty stupid way to handle things, but it's still a big improvement over what you would have done a few months ago. So cut yourself some slack. Now can we get out of here?"

"Yeah, I guess I best get goin'. I keep forgettin' that nowadays someone actually cares whether or not I come home."

We closed up the hole and I rode Tommy to his house on my bike.

"You want to hear something funny?" I asked. "Beau is a French word that means nice or attractive."

"Boy, did his parents ever get it wrong," Tommy replied.

Graduation Day: I

I have had playmates, I have had companions,
In my days of childhood, in my joyful school-days-
All, all are gone, the old familiar faces.
                    Old Familiar Faces by Charles Lamb

I awoke smiling but jittery on graduation day. Actually the school called it Commencement, but to me it was graduation. Ma had bought me a new suit and new shoes for the big day. Ma was feeling poorly again, tired and sick to her stomach. Her stomach virus just wouldn't go away. It had been coming and going for weeks. She was only worried that I would catch it and miss my big day. She was pale, but she insisted that she would not miss my graduation. Pa took off from work. Ma said,

"We'll pick up Grandma and Grandpa, and then we will meet you at school." I went early for the rehearsal. I looked for Becky because I had a present for her that I wanted to give her privately. I caught up with her in the gym.

"Becky, I brought your graduation gift. I thought you might want to wear it tonight." I handed her the little jewelry box. And she gasped when she opened the locket.

"Oh, I love it."

"Open it," I said. Inside was a picture of us at the New Year's Dance.

"What a perfect present. Now wherever I am, you'll be with me. Can you put it on me?" I stood behind her and fumbled with the catch. Then I reached over, put it around her neck, and hooked it. Looking to make sure no one was watching, I put my arms about her waist, and kissed her cheek. Then I quickly released her. I didn't dare do more than that in school. Mr. Stimson had suspended April just last month for necking in the halls. Of course that was before the rumors about her spread like wildfire through the school. Now no guy would touch her with a ten foot pole!

Becky told me she had my gift at her house, and I'd get it when I walked her home. She ran off to join the other girls and show off her locket. All the girls had autograph books or autograph dogs for the other students to sign. The boys just had friends sign their Commencement booklets. I'm not good at writing stuff, but in Becky's book I drew a picture of her and me and wrote one word, FOREVER. She really liked that. In Ted's booklet, I just wrote "To my old friend, Ted. See you next year in High School." I signed Tommy's book, "From one Bulb-head to another. I'll miss you next year. Good luck in O'Shea." Actually Tommy's hair had mostly grown back, but where the stitches had been, there was a bald spot. He had learned to comb his hair so the spot was barely noticeable. Fortunately I had the graduation cap to cover my bald head. When I read what Tommy wrote to me, I was really touched. "To Barry: my first friend. You taught me what friendship is. Thank you. I'll miss you next year." Becky's sign was kind of cute. "U and I 4ever."

As Tommy and I headed to the auditorium after picking up our caps and gowns, Beau Stuart brushed past Tommy with just enough of a bump to make it clear it wasn't an accident. He muttered "Rag Boy" under his breath.

I saw Tommy's hands curl into fists.

I shouted, "What's the matter with you Stuart? Do you have a death wish?"

Tommy's fists relaxed. He faced his nemesis.

"Your parents sure got it wrong when they named you. There is nothing beau about you." He and I exchanged high fives as we walked to line up for graduation.

The awards ceremony was the best part of the whole day. I got an award as the best overall student. And I received the art award, too. Tommy received one for most improved student. Becky got the Optimist Award for citizenship and community service. It was a good day for all the people I cared about.

All the girls were twittering about Miss Jenkins. She was wearing a big round diamond ring on her left hand. Becky gloated,

"I told you she'd be engaged before the end of the year!"

Miss Jenkins used one of my illustrations for the cover of the graduation booklet. Ma just about busted a gut with pride when she saw that. She bought extra copies of the booklet to send to every friend and relative in creation. Tommy and his mother got a standing ovation when they performed their song. But Graduation Day was bittersweet. We were all glad that we were moving on to high school, but a little scared, too. And Tommy was leaving.

Graduation Day: II

"Thee in an education grown of thee, in teachers, studies, students born of thee."
From *Thou Mother With Thy Equal Brood in* **Leaves of Grass** *by Walt Whitman*

It was graduation day. I awoke with butterflies in my stomach. For me, it was a real farewell, not just to grade school, but to New Hope. I was leaving the town and the school that had first rejected, and then embraced me. I was leaving my first real friend, and my first girlfriend.

Mama insisted that I get all decked out in my new suit and shoes. I argued that no one would see the clothes under the cap and gown, but there is no winnin' an argument with Mama. And I'm just so glad to have her back, I don't have the heart to fight with her much. So I went off to school like a real "Yankee Doodle Dandy," southern-style. Mama wanted to go to school with me, but I had to be there early for rehearsal, and she was waitin' for grandma and grandpa to drive in from O'Shea. Besides, I wanted to get there early. There were people I needed to see.

I wanted to talk to Cheryl alone, but she and her friends were busy runnin' around gettin' their autograph books signed. I did catch up with Barry, but we weren't alone. I signed his commencement book. No silly rhyme this time. I had to let him know what his friendship meant to me.

Before I knew it, Barry and I had to rush off to get our caps and gowns. As we left the gym and headed toward the auditorium, Beau Stuart rammed into me and muttered "Rag Boy." For a minute I nearly lost it. I felt my hands tighten into fists. But as Barry shouted at Beau, my fists just as quickly uncurled.

Instead, in as cutting a voice as I could muster, I said,

"Your parents sure got it wrong when they named you. There is nothing beau about you." As Barry and I continued toward the auditorium, he smiled at me and gave me a high five. No need for words. He was tellin' me he was proud of me, and I was kinda proud of me, too.

The ceremony was really neat. I was really glad when Barry won the award for Best Student and Becky won the Optimist Award. And of course, Barry got the Art Award. But you could have bowled me over with a feather when I won the Most Improved Student Award. In fact I was sorta daydreamin' when it was announced, and Barry had to practically push me put of my seat to go get it. I never won anything good before in my life. In fifth grade, the kids voted me "Most likely to land in jail." I sure hope no one noticed that my eyes misted over for a second.

And then Ma and me...I...sang our song, and the audience roared its approval. It just doesn't get any better than that.

THE HOSPITAL AGAIN: I

i thank You God for most this amazing day:...
this is the birthday of life and of love and wings
I Thank You God For Most This Amazing by E. E. Cummings

At the graduation party at the New Hope Diner, Tommy's mom told Ma,

"I love my friends here. Everyone has been so supportive. But I can't stay in New Hope. That was the home of Maggie Thompson. And Maggie Thompson no longer exists. I don't ever want to return to that house where I suffered such pain. I want Tommy to live in O'Shea, the town that nourished and sustained me as a child, the only place where I was truly happy. I want Tommy to get to know his grandparents." My Ma understood. She hugged Tommy's Ma.

"If you ever want to come back to visit, we have an extra bedroom in the house. We'd love to have you."

"And if your family wants to visit O'Shea, we have a guest house on the family estate that you can use. Tommy and I will be staying in it until our new home is finished, but then it will be available anytime."

Just then Ma's face turned white, and she fainted. She would have fallen, but my Pa was behind her in a second, and caught her in his arms. She came to in a minute, but she seemed dizzy and disoriented.

"That's it," said Pa. "You've been feeling poorly for weeks. We are going to the hospital right now." Ma started to protest.

"I'm fine Harry. I just got dizzy for a second. Really I'm fine." I could tell she was embarrassed about all the fuss. But Pa looked scared, and I had never seen him scared before.

"No arguments, Molly. You are going to the hospital."

Pa drove Ma to the emergency room. Tommy's Ma drove Tommy and Becky and me over. We'd spent a lot of time in the hospital this year, and I didn't look forward to walking in those doors again. Becky held my hand. She didn't say much which was unusual for her, but I was glad she was there. I was scared. I never thought of anything happening to my parents. Sure they were embarrassing sometimes, but they were always there for me. It couldn't be anything serious, could it? Ma wasn't that old.

The doctors had sent Pa out while they examined Ma. Pa was pacing the room. He was nervous and that made me nervous. Someone must have called Grandma and Grandpa. They'd gone back to our house to rest after the graduation ceremony. When they entered the waiting room, Grandpa was deathly pale. Grandma kept twisting her handkerchief in her hand. I don't think I'd ever seen them look so frail, unsteady, and scared. I helped them to a sofa. I brought them some tea from the waiting room lounge. Becky came into the room, and I barely realized she had been gone. I took her hand again.

Just then the doctor came in to talk to Pa. They went into Ma's. I followed them as far as Ma's doorway. I stared in after them from there. I watched Pa. When he walked in, he looked almost deflated, smaller than I'd ever seen him. But as the doctor spoke, Pa seemed to inflate again. Ma, too. Her cheeks went from chalk to blush in seconds. Pa kissed Ma right in front of the doctor. Then he strutted toward the doorway with the goofiest grin on his face.

"Uh, Barry, you know that baby brother you were always nagging us about. It seems you may finally get him."

"What?" What was I feeling? Anger? Relief? Disbelief? Embarrassment? Weren't they too old for that? Wasn't I too old for that?

"Your mother is due in six months," he boasted.

I was still dumbstruck and stood glued in the doorway. Pa kind of jerked his head toward Ma and I dutifully went in and kissed her. I didn't know what to say. I was still dazed when I went back to the waiting room. Grandma looked up, eyes wide. The handkerchief had disappeared. Now she was fumbling with her prayer beads. She stared at my face but couldn't seem to read it. And I couldn't quite get the words out because they still wouldn't register in my brain.

"Well," Grandpa snapped. "What did the doctor say?"

"She's… going to have a baby." I knew my face was beet red.

"Oh, thank You, Lord," exhaled Grandma.

"Well, then why are you looking so somber, Boy? You scared the devil out of us!"

"It takes some getting used to," I whispered. Becky put her hand on my arm.

"Didn't you tell me not long ago that you wanted a baby brother? So why the long face?"

"You know that old saying: 'Be careful what you wish for because you might get it.' Well now I understand what it means! Besides there's no guarantee that it will be a boy."

Pa came into the room grinning like a fool to hugs and back slaps from everyone in the waiting room. Tommy said to me,

"Congratulations, Big Brother. I'm sorry I won't be here to see you changing diapers!"

"Yeah, thanks!"

"Seriously, this baby is lucky. You'll make a great Big Brother. And I know what I'm talkin' 'bout 'cause you're the closest thing I ever had to a brother."

"Ditto."

"Listen, since the news is good, Ma and I are going to head back to the Graduation Party. There are some people I want to say goodbye to." I looked at Pa. He was still grinning his fool head off.

"Go ahead," he said. "It's your day and you earned it. We're very proud of you. I'll take Ma home to rest and you come home when the party is over."

THE HOSPITAL AGAIN: II

Here is the deepest secret nobody knows
(here is the root of the root and the bud of the bud…)
I Carry Your Heart With Me by E.E. Cummings

At the graduation party at the New Hope Diner, my Mama told Mrs. Brenner,

"I love my friends here. Everyone has been so supportive. But I can't stay in New Hope. That was the home of Maggie Thompson. And Maggie Thompson no longer exists. I don't ever want to return to that house where I suffered such pain. I want Tommy to live in O'Shea, the town that nourished and sustained me as a child, the only place where I was truly happy. I want Tommy to get to know his grandparents better."

I had mixed feelings. Life in New Hope hadn't been a picnic for me, but it was the only home I knew. I was just startin' to get friends here. I'd hafta leave Cheryl and Barry. But Mama loved O'Shea so. And it sure was nice havin' grandparents who wanted to spoil me. And in O'Shea I could start fresh. I had no past history to overcome. Still…

Mrs. Brenner hugged Mama.

"If you ever want to come back to visit, we have an extra bedroom in the house. We'd love to have you."

"And if your family wants to visit O'Shea, we have a guest house on the family estate that you can use. Tommy and I will be staying in it until our new home is finished, but then it will be available anytime."

I was gettin' ready to talk to Cheryl. It would be hard to say goodbye. But just then Mrs. Brenner turned whiter than a sheet, and she dropped like a stone. Mr. Brenner caught her in his arms. She came to in a minute, but she seemed kinda out of it. Mr. Brenner said something about her feelin' poorly for weeks. He insisted on takin' her to the hospital. I could tell she was embarrassed about all the fuss, but off they went. I forgot about the party or talkin' to Cheryl. I couldn't find her to explain what had happened, but I couldn't wait. Barry had been there for me when Mama was in the hospital. I had to do the same for him. Mama drove Barry and me and Rebecca to the emergency room. I hated entering that place again. I knew just how Barry felt in that waitin' room not knowin' how his Ma was doin'. I told him,

"She'll be okay. They doctors and nurses here are the best. Trust me on that."

"I know." But he didn't seem at all convinced. His Pa paced the room like a caged tiger. Between him and the blond man waitin' for his baby to be born, they near wore out the carpet.

I din't know what to say or do, but Rebecca did. She held his hand for dear life. I was glad she was there for him. Then Barry's grandparents came in. I knew they were old, but between the graduation ceremony and now, they'd aged another twenty years. Barry kept himself busy gettin' chairs and drinks for them. I was glad. It kept his mind off the wait. Sometime during that Rebecca disappeared. I din't know she was gone, till she came back.

"You Ma will be all right," Rebecca asserted. "There's a chapel down the hall. I just lit a candle for her." Her calm assurance was just what Barry needed.

"Thanks! That was nice of you." Barry seemed relieved. I wish't I'd thought to do that, but then church hadn't been part of my life much in the last seven years.

The doctor called Mr. Brenner to his wife's bedside. Barry followed behind. Those of us in the waitin' room got real quiet. There isn't much to say at a time like that. Still I couldn't ever remember Rebecca bein' that quiet. Mama was talkin' to Barry's grandparents. I asked them and Mama and Rebecca if they wanted somethin' from the cafeteria. But nobody could eat.

When Barry came back he had the strangest look on his face. I din't know how to read him. He seemed relieved and scared and angry and confused all at the same time. He opened his mouth and then closed it again. He looked like the words were jumblin' round in his head, and he couldn't get them out. His Grandpa finally snapped,

"Well, what did the doctor say?"

Red-faced, Barry stammered, "Ma's going to have a baby."

"Well, then why are you looking so somber, Boy? You scared the devil out of us!"

"It takes some getting used to," Barry whispered. Becky put her hand on his arm.

"Didn't you tell me not long ago that you wanted a baby brother? So why the long face?"

"You know that old saying: 'Be careful what you wish for because you might get it.' Well now I understand what it means! Besides there's no guarantee that it will be a boy."

Barry's Pa came into the room grinning like the Cheshire cat. He hugged and received back slaps from everyone in the waiting room. He and the still-pacing expectant father shook hands.

"Congratulations, Big Brother," I told Barry. "I'm sorry I won't be here to see you changing diapers!"

"Yeah, thanks!"

"Seriously, this baby is lucky. You'll make a great Big Brother. And I know what I'm talkin' 'bout 'cause you're the closest thing I ever had to a brother."

"Ditto."

"Listen, since the news is good, Ma and I are going to head back to the Graduation Party. There are some people I want to say goodbye to."

"Thanks for being here for me. I was really scared."

"I know. Believe me I know."

Barry's dad told him to run along and enjoy the rest of the party, so Mama drove the three of us back to the diner. But by the time I got there, Cheryl had left. Someone told her what happened, and she figured I'd be at the hospital with Barry all night. I just had to see her again before I left for O'Shea.

FAREWELL: I

"Parting is such sweet sorrow."
Romeo and Juliet *by William Shakespeare*

On their last day in town, there was a church service of farewell for Tommy and his Ma. Tommy attended. So did I. I saw Tommy's eyes widen when I entered the church without my cap. He knew what that had cost me, and he knew I had done it for him. I could see that in his eyes. He'd never admit it, and I'll never tell anyone, but I could see tears welling. The service was really nice. The Priest talked about maturity and friendship and strength in adversity. Then the choir sang. Cheryl had a sweet little voice, but I absolutely got goosebumps when Becky did her solo.

When the service was over, the sisterhood had a nice luncheon. There was a farewell cake and sandwiches. I kept looking for Tommy. He and Cheryl disappeared for a while. I could only guess how hard that goodbye was for him. I know I couldn't bear it if I had to say goodbye to Becky. Finally they reappeared. Cheryl looked like she had been crying. Tommy didn't look so hot either. I was about to go to him, when his Ma sent him to talk to Miss Jenkins. Hard to believe she won't be Miss Jenkins when school starts again in September. Mr. Faulkner is a lucky man.

Finally, I gave up looking for Tommy. I went out and sat on the steps of the church. Outside, I could've put my cap back on, but I didn't. I just sat there and thought. I understood why Tommy and his Ma wanted to leave, but I was sorry to see Tommy go. We had taken a torturous route to friendship, and I didn't want to see it end. Finally Tommy came out and sat beside me on the step.

"What, no cap?"

"Nah. What's the point? It's not like it's a secret. Everyone already knows I'm bald. And no one seems to care much except me."

We exchanged addresses and phone numbers.

"I'll write," he promised.

"I'll visit during summer vacation," I insisted. But I think we both knew that we wouldn't.

Farewell: II

I come to you as a grown child
Who has had a pig-headed father;
I am old enough now to make friends.

A Pact by Ezra Pound

It was my last day in New Hope. I was nervous about movin.' Din't know how it would be startin' a new school in a new town, without knowin' anybody. In New Hope Elementary the eighth graders were kings of the school. But next year I'd be a freshman in O'Shea High School, low man on the totem pole. It's always tough bein' the youngest, but bein' the youngest without friends, that really put my stomach in knots. Mama said to introduce myself as Tommy O'Shea Thompson, cause bein' an O'Shea counts for a lot in town.

The church had a farewell service and luncheon just for me and Mama. It was the first time I'd been in a church in seven years. I had a lot of confessing to do. When the collection plate came around, it felt good to be able to pull money out of my pocket to put in it. I knew the church used some of the money to feed the poor, cause in previous years Snake and me and been the recipients of those nameless food baskets that sometimes showed up on our front stoop.

I looked around the room. Most of the kids from school were there. Miss Jenkins was there glowing and smiling, on the arm of Mr. Faulkner. Come August, she woun't be Miss Jenkins anymore. But my eyes nearly brimmed over when I saw the Brenners there with Barry. I knew how much it took for him to come with his bald head exposed, and I knew he did it for me.

Cheryl and Rebecca were in the choir. Cheryl had a sweet little voice, but Rebecca was amazing. That girl could purely sing. Cheryl looked at me while she sang, and there were tears in her eyes. I felt some stinging my eyes but I refused to let them fall.

At the luncheon, I pulled Cheryl aside. I had a present for her. Mama helped me pick it out. Since she played the violin in the school orchestra, I got her a little gold violin charm for her charm bracelet. We sneaked into the organ room and kissed, long and hard. She hugged me and I felt somethin' stirrin' in me. I din't know whether to hug her like there was no tomorrow, or run out of the room to get my feelin's under control. Cheryl was cryin' full out. I stroked her hair. I held her. It felt good and a little scary all at the same time.

"I'll write. I'll call. You can come to visit."

"Sure," she said, but she didn't sound sure at all.

"Besides, you'll be busy at band camp all summer. Even if I stayed in New Hope, I woun't see you."

"But I'd know you'd be there when I came home."

"Tommy? Where are you?" It was my Mama's voice callin'.' I released Cheryl, and wiped her tears with my handkerchief. I took her hand and pulled her back into the main hall.

"Here, this is for you." I stuffed a piece of paper in her hand.

"What is it?"

"It's the song I wrote for you." Her eyes filled up again.

"What are you cryin' for? It's not that bad, is it?" Before she could answer, Mama came up to us.

"There you are Tommy. Miss Jenkins is getting ready to leave. Did you give her the gift?"

"Not yet, Mama."

"Well go on then." I looked at Cheryl who appeared ready to burst into tears again. Mama noticed, too, and she put her arm around Cheryl.

"Go on, now. I'll take care of your friend here."

"Miss Jenkins, could you wait one minute. I have something for you." I held out the wrapped present.

"Why, Tommy, how thoughtful of you. That wasn't necessary. Thank you."

"Yes, Ma'am. It was necessary. You were the first teacher who din't think I was dumb."

"You keep up your writing now. Someday when you are famous, I'll be able to tell the world that I was the first teacher who recognized your talent." She opened the box and smiled in that way that made her nose crinkle up. I knew that meant she liked it. She took the red marble apple out of the box.

"You couldn't have gotten me anything that I would love more. This will be on my desk every day, so I'll always remember you. Will I embarrass you if I give you a hug?" She did, before I had a chance to answer.

"Thank you, Miss Jenkins... and ...um... Good luck to you and Mr. Faulkner."

"Thank you, Tommy."

The party was breaking up and I still hadn't talked to Barry. I found him on the front step of the church, without his cap. I think he's gonna be okay with the bulb-head thing. We shook hands.

"Good luck in O'Shea," Barry began. "I know why you have to go, but I still wish you wouldn't. I'll miss you."

"I'll miss you, too. You were my first friend. Thanks for stickin' by me even when I was a jerk."

"No problem."

"I'll write you. And you can visit me in O'Shea you know. There's plenty of room for company."

"Yeah, maybe I will." But I think we both knew he wouldn't.

Epilogue

▼

Darest thou now O soul,
Walk out with me toward the unknown region.
Darest Thou Now O Soul from **Leaves of Grass** *by Walt*
Whitman

It's summer again, hazy, hot and humid. Tommy is gone. I work in Pa's store in the mornings. Most afternoons, I go to the watering hole with Ted and the other boys. And Saturday nights, Becky and I go to the movies or bowling. The trip to Florida was a dream-come-true. Snorkeling at Pennekamp Park made my mind up for me for sure. I want to be a marine biologist.

This time last year, I was a self-centered child, innocent and immature. My baldness was the main focus of my existence. Somewhere during the past nine months, world circumstances, human nature, and personal experience made me grow up. I lost my innocence, but I gained perspective. I am still bald, probably always will be, but it's okay. From my friendships with Tommy and Becky, and the missile crisis, I learned to look beyond myself to see what is important. I watch the news regularly now. The country has turned optimistic again, with the missile crisis behind us and the space program taking off. I think the 1963-1964 school year will bring a better time for America, for New Hope, and for me.

Questions for Discussion

1. This story is set in 1962. The Cuban Missile Crisis framed Barry's reality. What current world or national events affect how you view the world?

2. Many teenagers have things that they wish they could change, so they could feel better about themselves. Why does Barry feel self-conscious? Why does Tommy feel like an outsider at school? Why doesn't Becky seem confident about herself in the beginning of the book?

3. Are there things about yourself that you wouldn't want friends to know or that you don't like about yourself?

4. Did you ever feel like an outsider, different from your classmates? Do you still feel that way? How did you handle those feelings? If you no longer feel different or isolated, what changed?

5. How did Barry change from the beginning of the book to the end? What events in his life helped bring about that change?

6. How did Tommy change from the beginning of the book to the end? What events in his life helped to bring about that change?

7. Why does Tommy tease Barry at the beginning of the book? Why does he continue to tease him even after Barry is nice to him?

8. How does Rebecca change during the course of the book? Why?

9. How does Miss Jenkins help Tommy and Barry change?

10. Have you ever had a teacher like Miss Jenkins? How did that teacher help you?

11. Have you ever escaped your problems in fantasies? Does it help?

12. Why does Barry escape into fantasies at the beginning of the book?

13.   Why do you think the fantasies disappear by the end of the book?

14.   What special talents do Barry, Becky, Cheryl and Tommy have?

15.   How do those talents help influence events in the story?

16.   What special talents do you have?

17.   Which characters in the book would you like to have as friends? Why?

18.   Which characters would you not want as friends? Why?

19.   Do you know a student like Tommy at the beginning of the book? What do you know about the family/home life of that person? How do you deal with that person? What do you think that person will be like 5-10 years from now?

20.   Why do you think April behaves the way she does?

21.   Do you know a student like April? How do you deal with her?

22.   If you wrote a sequel to this book set in 1970, what do you think each of the characters would be doing?

23.   Are the characters in this book different from students the same age today? If so, how?

24.   How can you tell when Barry is relating the story and when Tommy is telling his version?

25.   How do the fantasy sequences differ from the rest of the book?

26.   Just by looking at the dialogue, how can you tell when Barry is speaking and when Tommy is speaking?

27.   Just by looking at the dialogue, can you tell when Becky is speaking and when Cheryl is speaking? How?

28.   What did you think about this book? What parts of the book did you like? What parts didn't you like? Why?

29.   Did any part of this book remind you of your own life? Explain.

30.   What did you learn by reading this book?

31.   What do you want to know about the plot, setting, characters that the book did not tell you?

Research Topics

1. Research the Space program in the 1960's

    What was the Mercury Program?

    What was the Apollo program?

    What is a L.E.M.?

    When did Houston Space Center open up?

    When did man first land on the moon?

2. What everyday tools, gadgets, appliances, and toys commonly used today were not available in 1962? What did kids use then that they don't use now?

    What is a skate key?

    How do you shoot bottle caps?

    How do you play Chinese jump rope?

    What is a typewriter?

    What is a 45 record?

    What do teens today use or do instead of using or doing the things mentioned above?

3. Research the presidency of John F. Kennedy.

4. Research the Bay of Pigs Invasion.

5. Research the Cuban Missile Crisis.

6.   Research one of the poets quoted at the start of one of this book's chapters. Focus particularly on Ezra Pound, Robert Frost, Emily Dickinson, E.E. Cummings, or Walt Whitman.

7.   Learn more about Alopecia.

Author Interview

Q. When did you start writing?

A. I stared writing poetry when I was 7. I really got hooked on writing in 5th grade when a short story I wrote got published in my class newspaper. Then in Jr. High, I was the poetry editor of the award-winning school magazine *Fels Chips*.

I was first paid for writing when I wrote an article for *Highlights i*n 1980. After that I co-wrote several textbooks.

Q. Where do you get the ideas for your books?

A. From observing and listening to people around me, especially children. This book title originated in a comment my daughter made at the age of five. She meant to say someone was bald-headed, but she mispronounced it "bulb-headed." I filed the phrase away in my memory until I decided to write this story about a bulb-headed boy. My story *Achoo Choo Choo*(Sept. 2007 *Highlights High Five Magazine)* came from watching my grandson Hunter playing with a train, when he suddenly sneezed. I thought: Wouldn't it be funny if a train said "Achoo" instead of "Choo Choo"? *Broccoliosaur Stories* came from my grandson Nicholas who said a brachiosaurus should be called a "broccoliosaurus" because "He eats broccoli."

Q. Why did you set the book in 1962?

A. Because I've always been told I should write about what I know. I was a young teenager in 1962. I remember the fear during the Cuban Missile Crisis, and like Barry, I stocked a closet as a bomb shelter in the basement of my home. And because I think today's readers who lived through 9/11 can relate to the characters' reactions to the missile crisis.

Q. What makes a good writer?

A. Reading! Reading! Reading! Almost all good authors I know started out as children who loved to read. Imagination, observation skills, and basic grammar, research, and a willingness to revise, are all important, but first a writer must love books.